DOWNSIDE UP

Hayley Long was born in Ipswich ages ago. She studied English at university in Wales, where she had a very nice time and didn't do much work. After that she spent several years in various places abroad and had a very nice time and didn't do much work then either. Now Hayley is an English teacher and works very hard indeed. She lives in Norwich with a rabbit called Irma and a husband.

Other books by Hayley Long

Lottie Biggs Is NOT Mad
Lottie Biggs Is NOT Desperate
Lottie Biggs Is NOT Tragic
What's Up with Jody Barton?

DOWNSIDE UP

Hayley Long

MACMILLAN CHILDREN'S BOOKS

First published 2013 by Macmillan Children's Books
a division of Macmillan Publishers Limited
20 New Wharf Road, London N1 9RR
Basingstoke and Oxford
Associated companies throughout the world
www.panmacmillan.com

ISBN 978-1-4472-2008-4

1 3 5 7 9 8 6 4 2

A CIP catalogue record for this book is available from
the British Library.

Printed and bound by CPI Group (UK) Ltd, Croydon CR0 4YY

For the Barefoot Executive

'I can't go back to yesterday because I was a different person then.'

– Lewis Carroll, *Alice's Adventures in Wonderland*

Ronni Runnacles @ronneee_r

I've got some seriously freaky things to tell you. #wheretostart?

Most stories start once upon a time, a long time ago. But not this one. This is a story about what happened yesterday.

Then again, it's about some other stuff too. And some of that other stuff happened in the days and weeks leading up to yesterday. So maybe I need to backtrack a bit more and begin one month ago. On the day that my dad left.

That was also the day I got into a fight.

I'm not just talking about a few shouty words and a shove. Or a scrap or a spat or a bust-up or a scuffle or anything like that. I'm talking about a proper, no-messing, claws-out, teeth-bared, hackles rattled, full-on, battle for survival.

Sort of like *The Hunger Games* but in a food-technology classroom.

One moment I was stirring flour into my Victoria-sponge cake mix, and the next I'd scooped up a huge handful of unbaked slop and hurled it as hard as I could at Sadie Slowgrove's head.

It's fair to say I wasn't having a good day.

Within half a second, everyone had rushed from their workstations and clotted together in a shrinking circle round us. Some people were waving wooden spoons and others were banging on saucepans and loads more were holding up their phones and taking photos and all of them were screaming and shrieking and laughing and cheering and chanting . . .

'Fight! Fight! Fight!'

And at the same time, they were pushing and shoving and bundling and moshing and crushing in as close as they could just to get the best view of me and Sadie Slowgrove as we tried our hardest to rip each other's hair out.

Afterwards, Stuart Bolan – who everyone fancies – put the whole thing on YouTube. YouTube took it straight off again.

But I wound up in a whole heap of grief anyway. For starters, I was made to sit outside the Headteacher's office and told to write down exactly what had happened. But I couldn't. I just kept stopping and starting and scrunching up endless pieces of paper, and instead of thinking about Sadie Slowgrove and the food-tech fight, I kept on thinking about my mum and about how I'd found her, earlier that same morning, just sitting on our kitchen floor and crying. And then I started thinking about my dad and how I'd gone to bed the night before believing that everything in my life was okey-dokey and Diet-Cokey and how I now knew that – actually – it wasn't.

In the end I hardly wrote a word. I just sat there. Some things are really difficult to explain. Throwing cake mix into somebody's face is one of them.

And then there was that lie I told in the lesson. How do I explain that? I know *why* I lied. I lied because I couldn't handle telling the truth. But why *that* lie? It was as random as the pepper I'd accidentally shaken into my beaten eggs, margarine and sugar.

It was supposed to have been my dad's birthday cake, by the way. Because the day he left us was his birthday.

My eyes were fixed on my wooden spoon and I was whirling it faster and faster through the pointless plop in my bowl. Dimly in the background somewhere, I heard Mrs Duncan – my food-tech teacher – shouting, 'Make sure you're *folding* your flour and not beating it to death, please.' And then – much nearer and clearer – I heard my best friend, Flooky, say, 'Are you all right, Ronni? You seem well tense.'

And my other best friend, Kelly Bugg, said, 'Is something on your mind?'

And because I didn't want to say, 'Yes actually. My family is a complete car crash,' I shook my head and said something else instead. This:

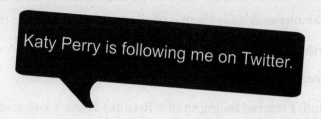

Katy Perry is following me on Twitter.

It's weird because I hadn't been thinking about Katy Perry at all. I hadn't even been thinking about Twitter.

My friends stopped what they were doing and looked at me amazed.

And then Flooky said, 'What? The actual Katy Perry? Or just some random Katy Perry who works in Argos?'

And straight away, I said, 'The verified Katy Perry.'

Flooky went quiet for a second. Then she snorted into her buttercream filling and said, 'Yeah, right! And pigs might fly!'

Kelly Bugg put down her whisk and said, 'No offence, yeah, but it is quite hard to believe. Last time I looked at Twitter, you only had seven followers. And two of them are us.'

And straight away, I replied, 'Yeah, but have you seen who the other five are? They're all celebrities. I'm being followed by the tweet elite.'

Flooky and Kelly Bugg looked at each other. Then they burst out laughing.

And even though I wasn't in any kind of laughing mood, *I* started laughing too. Because I didn't know what else to do. So all three of us just stood there and split our sides over the fact that I was such a freaky random liar.

Sometimes you have to laugh or else you'd cry.

But then I looked over to the next workstation and I saw that Sadie Slowgrove was laughing too. And straightaway, I stopped laughing and *almost* did start crying. I didn't though. Instead, I put on this brand-new tough face that I never knew I had, raised my chin up really high and said loudly, 'Er . . . Excuse me. What the heck d'you think you're laughing at, Sadie Slowgrove?'

There was so much noise from all the food-mixers and fan ovens and general chit-chat that Mrs Duncan didn't hear me.

But Sadie Slowgrove did. She looked at me, raised her eyebrows and said, 'Was I actually laughing at you? Was I actually even aware you were there?'

And, to be honest, there's a fair chance that the answer to her first question was actually No. But she knew I was there all right. No doubt about it.

So I just kept on glaring and said, 'I flipping well saw you talking about me behind your hand.'

Sadie Slowgrove stared back at me. And then she said, 'Liar.'

And for some reason that was the thin end of the wedge. I threw down my wooden spoon and said, 'Why don't you just crawl back under your rock and disappear. And while you're about it, tell your mum to disappear as well.'

From the corner of my eye, I could tell that Flooky and Kelly Bugg were looking pretty stunned. I'm not surprised. This mouthy new me was probably a shock to everyone.

Sadie Slowgrove's face turned toxic and she stood up from her stool and said, 'It's not my flipping fault that your dad is a moron.'

And that was when I let her have it with the cake mix.

That all happened one month ago. Me and Sadie Slowgrove have kept right out of each other's way since then. Mostly, I've kept right out of everyone else's way too.

And I mean **everyone.**

It's been a bit like this.

I've been here.

Me.

And everyone else has been on an entirely different page.

My brothers.

My mum.

My nan.

Even my best friends, Flooky and Kelly Bugg, have been a little way off.

Not in terms of actual distance perhaps. But in terms of headspace I've been floating around in my own separate galaxy. And it's a galaxy where my dad doesn't walk with me along the seafront any more. And he doesn't give me all his 2ps for the 2p coin-shove machines. Or buy me chips that come in a cone of rolled-up newspaper. Or sit next to me on the sea-wall watching the waves. Or race me round and round the dodgem track until he's got no money left.

In fact, it's a galaxy where it's easier to pretend that he doesn't exist.

And, just lately, I've been pretending a load of other stuff too. While I've been wrapped up in my duvet or staring out of classroom windows or making my baby brother's tea, I've been pretending to be someone else.

But now – at last – I *am* someone else. At least, I'm definitely not the same person I was yesterday morning. I've changed. And it's all because of this very,

very

weɹd

thing

that happened yesterday afternoon.

In fact, it was SO weird that I'm not sure you're even going to believe it when I tell you. I wouldn't blame you if you didn't. I'm struggling to believe it all myself.

But what I do know is that something happened yesterday which made me see the world in a completely different way. And I'm going to take you right back to the start of that day. When I wasn't seeing *anything*. Because I hadn't even opened my eyes . . .

Under the cover of darkness, I switched off the real world and flicked to a channel that was way more interesting.

I was in a strange place. It was a place which had no noisy brothers and no red-eyed mum and no nagging nan. In this place, everyone was wearing a security pass and a T-shirt with my face on it. In this place, everyone was really cool.

'Now *this* . . .' I said to myself, '. . . is much more my scene!'

My heels twitched with excitement and I heard an unfamiliar clinking sound. Glancing down, I saw that I was standing on a metal disc plonked – like a stepping stone – in a field of mud. I lifted my gaze again. Towers of scaffolding were everywhere. They reached up to a high ceiling that covered an area at least as large as a decent shopping centre. In this enormous, dark, muddy space, people were rushing about in every direction and shouting into headsets and handsets and loudhailers. The only people who weren't rushing around was a group of dancers in black leotards. They were standing together on mud-splattered gym mats and doing some complicated stretching exercises.

I watched them for a second or two and then I called over, 'Hey, y'all better get your freak on, sisters!'

The dancers stopped stretching and their eyes widened with respect. Then the tallest and coolest of them nodded at me and said, 'You sure can count on us, girrrrl! You *know* that!'

And I nodded fiercely and said, 'I damn well DO know it, girlfriend.'

And I *did* as well. Because I was Miss Ronni Runaway and everyone wanted to be me.

Above us, music began to play. It was so loud that I could feel every single beat thump through my body. It was just like those prickly little shocks you sometimes get from your school jumper. I closed my eyes and took a couple of slow deep breaths to help me focus.

In . . . Out . . . In . . . Out . . .

And then I opened my eyes again and winked. But it wasn't just any old wink. It was the wink that meant I was ready to get this party started.

Someone shouted, 'Time to get a shift on!'

There was a clunk and a whirring noise below me. The metal disc beneath my feet trembled.

Someone shouted, 'Just stand real still!'

Slowly, I began to rise up and up – away from the mud and the dancers and the people with their headsets and handsets and loudhailers. And I kept on rising up and up and up until I was moving through a round hole cut into the ceiling.

And then I found myself on a massive stage.

A spotlight shone into my eyes and a strange noise filled the air. For a moment, I couldn't work out what it was. It was a bit like the sound of a plane taking off. Or the sound of a billion birds all perched in the exact same tree. Or the roar of a hurricane passing overhead.

But then I realized it was the sound of one hundred and thirty-five thousand individual people starting to cheer.

And they were all cheering me.

I could see them in front of me. It was as if the entire world had turned into one great big sea of waving arms and floating flags and flashing camera lenses.

My heels twitched with excitement. Then I shook back my hair, wiggled my hips and began to sing. And the crowd erupted.

I felt fantastic.

I felt electric.

I felt totally and utterly amazing!

And then I stopped singing and shouted,

'Glastonbury . . . Are you ready?'

And I guess they were because the crowd in front of me just went

damn straight insane.

So I wiggled my hips again and fed them a line from my groundbreaking, award-winning, international Number One hit single.

'Roll up your sleeves, pull up your socks –
Cos I'm still Ronni from the docks.'

And the crowd joined in and started singing along and it was clear that they were absolutely loving me. And, to be perfectly honest, *I* was absolutely loving me too – because I was wearing an amazing pair of gold high-heeled boots and a matching gold jacket and shorts so short that my nan would have choked on her chewy toffees.

Out of the main spotlight, I could feel the love coming at me from my backing dancers. And in the VIP enclosure I could feel the love coming at me from Beyoncé and Jay-Z and that man from Coldplay. I could feel the love everywhere.

So I blew a kiss to the crowd and chanted,

'What's my name? What's my name? What's my name . . . ?'

And, just like one single living breathing being, they all opened up their lungs and shouted . . .

Veronica Runnacles, GET UP NOW!'

The TV screen inside my head went fuzzy with interference, froze for a moment and then went blank. And into this sudden emptiness popped my first proper thought of the day. It was this:

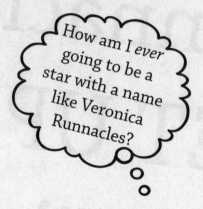

PFFF!

And close behind it was another thought:

How am I ever going to be a star with a name like Veronica Runnacles?

It was a pretty bleak way to wake up. But then I remembered that Sadie Slowgrove isn't exactly a sexy name either. And neither is Kelly Bugg. And neither is Flooky – whose real name is actually Frida van der Flugt but nobody can pronounce it.

I groaned, rubbed the sleep out of my eyes and dragged my body into a sitting position. Then, stretching out an arm, I tugged back the curtain next to my bed and looked outside.

Just like I do every morning.

And all I could see was a . . .

BIG GREY WATERY SPLODGE

I wiped the window with my arm, yawned and had another look.

It was raining. In June. And it wasn't damp or drizzly or misty or spitting. This was proper actual bucketing rain and it was falling in poker-straight lines and bouncing off the big grey paving slabs in our backyard. Even the weather was harshing my mood.

'This is *so* not my scene,' I muttered. And then I looked at the world on the other side of our fence. Through the hammering rain, I could see grey cars and lorries rushing along all four lanes of the grey dual carriageway that goes all the way to the grey North Sea and then stops.

'Whoop,' I muttered.

I looked across to the other side of the road. Looming out of the early-morning mist, I could make out the shapes of hundreds of office blocks and thousands of big metal boxes. I watched as one of the boxes was hoisted upward by a crane, swung slowly through the air and loaded on to a massive grey ship. It was a sight I'd woken up to a million times before. Some places are famous for having Empire State Buildings and Eiffel Towers and Grand Canyons and gondoliers. But the place I live in is famous for having a really massive dock.

'Whoop,' I said again.

Plonking my elbows on the window ledge, I propped my chin on my hands, pushed my nose flat against the glass and searched the skyline until I spotted a small jet of orange flame flickering from the top of a tall metal pipe. And then – satisfied that it was still there – I let go of the curtain, flumped back down on my bed and closed my eyes.

'Ronni! Time to get a shift on. You'll be late for school!'

It was my mum. She was calling me from downstairs. She sounded vexed. But I knew she wasn't **really** that vexed. Otherwise she wouldn't have binned the last three letters the school had sent her about my late detentions.

So I didn't get moving. What was the point?

My mum's voice screamed up the stairs again. 'For God's sake, GET UP!'

I froze. And then I snuggled down further under my duvet. I know I shouldn't have done, but it felt like the best place to be.

Sleepiness and snugness and warmth washed over me. In the dark space behind my eyelids, a few festival flags came into focus.

'Mum says you've gotta get up!'

The flags vanished. I flipped back the top of my duvet and shouted, 'Ryan, get the heck OUT of my bedroom!'

Brother Number One – Ryan – is one of those kids

that everybody likes. He's got tufty black hair and a cute dimply face and he gets on well with everyone. My mum, my nan, my other brothers, other kids, teachers . . . they all love Ryan James Runnacles. The only person who ever seems to find him remotely annoying is me. He was leaning against my door frame with his arms folded. And instead of looking cute and dimply and lovable, he looked like a big fat irritating smugster.

There was a second of silence. And then he turned to the door and shouted, 'Muuuuum – she won't budge!' And after that, he said, 'You're setting such a bad example.'

'Oh, act your age,' I snapped. 'You're eleven! Not a hundred and eleven. Go and pop your spots.'

Ryan glared at me for a moment. Then – his face screwed up with concentration – he tensed his entire body before relaxing again with a big satisfied, 'Ahhhh!' And then he smirked and said, 'I bet you won't want to stay in bed now. I've just guffed. And it was a real ripper.'

For a second, I was so disgusted I went into a state of total shock. Then I picked up my pillow, hurled it right across the room at him and screamed . . .

'Get out!'

Ryan laughed. 'Mmmm . . . smells sweeeeet in here.' And then he slammed my door and ran off down the stairs.

I pulled the duvet back over my head and lay completely still. I was nearly crying. This is not how I like to wake up. It really isn't. Feeling around in the darkness, my fingers skipped over a book, three socks, a tube of lip balm and an empty crisp packet. And then they found my phone. I pulled it up to my face, pressed a button to illuminate the screen and wrote

 Ronni Runnacles @ronneee_r
Can my day get any worse???

I pressed Tweet. Straight away, a voice said, 'C'mon, lady, shift your carcass!'

It wasn't Ryan. It wasn't my mum either. I groaned out loud. And then I said, 'Oh, *Nan*! Can't I just have five more minutes?'

'No,' replied my nan. As if to confirm this fact, my duvet disappeared.

'Oh, *what*?' I sat up so fast that my eyesight went funny. I rubbed my eyes, frowned at my nan and said, 'What the flipping heck are you doing? Give me my duvet back!'

'Oi, oi, oi! Watch your language,' said my nan. 'I don't want to hear any of that effing and jeffing from you, lady. So wash your mouth out.'

My mouth fell open. For a second, I couldn't speak and then I said, 'How . . . how am I effing and jeffing? Since when has *flipping heck* been a swear word? I'm just expressing my valid opinion that this is completely unfair! You've got no right to barge in like this and steal my duvet. It's a total infringement of my basic human rights!'

My nan looked at me. Her eyes and lips had gone very narrow. Finally, she said, 'Is that so?'

'Yes,' I said. But I was already starting to feel a bit less sure.

My nan's eyes and lips went even narrower. I groaned out loud again.

My nan put her head on one side and said, 'I see. So let me ask you something, lady.'

I sighed and wished I could press a button and switch my nan to MUTE.

My nan said, 'How about your mum's basic human rights? Doesn't she have the right to live in this house without the school sending her letters every other day just because you can't be bothered to get your bones out of bed in time? And what about your brothers' human rights? Don't they have the right to live in this house without pussyfooting around an older sister who's got a bigger attitude than Genghis Khan? And what about my human rights? Don't I have the—'

'OK, OK, I get the flipping picture,' I said. 'I'm getting up.' And then – because I probably *do* have a bigger attitude than Genghis Khan – I added, 'There was no need to steal my duvet though. That was just rude.'

My nan dumped my duvet back on to my bed and sat down next to me. 'Well, in that case, you tell me how I'm supposed to get you up? Seriously, Ronni, I'd love to know. You don't set your alarm clock. You ignore your mum. You ignore Ryan when he tries to help. What else am I supposed to do? I'm sick of this, Ronni, I really am. It's not like you. You were as good as gold before your dad went. I know you're angry and I know you're upset, but the way you're behaving isn't making things any easier. Your poor mum is pulling her hair out.'

'Well, that's not my fault,' I said.

My nan frowned. 'Have you thought about what she's going through?'

'Yes,' I mumbled. And then I sighed very noisily and said, 'I can't exactly avoid it, can I?'

My nan didn't say anything to that.

I said, 'I'm sorry. Can you go now, please? I need to get up.'

My nan raised her eyebrows and smiled. 'No trouble at all.' And then she patted me on the arm and left my room.

And that pretty much sums up my nan. She's loud and tough and has spiky copper hair and big hoopy earrings. And she wears clothes that are slightly too tight with necklines that are slightly too low and she wears fancy tights and high-heeled shoes and she's so impossibly tricky and crafty and impossible to argue with that you always end up begging to do the one thing that you were fighting against in the first place.

I sat on the side of my bed and psyched myself up for the day ahead. Downstairs, I heard Ryan shout, 'Bye,' and then the front door slam shut. Unlike me, Ryan is never late for school. Not ever. Not even with all the chaos that's been going on. He still manages to get himself up and out of the house on time. I suppose it wouldn't bother me if we went to different schools, but we don't. Now that he's old enough, we go to the same one. And all the teachers think that he's cute and lovely and perfect and that I'm just a douchebag.

Seconds later, a car horn honked. There were more voices downstairs and more shouts of 'Bye' and the front door slammed again.

Suddenly the house got a whole lot quieter.

I stood up, crossed my room and headed across the landing to the bathroom. It's my second-favourite place in the house. Recently, I've acquired this habit of locking the door, filling the bath up to the top and spending absolutely ages in there and refusing point blank to come out.

To be honest, this was pretty much my plan for the entire morning.

But as I put my hand on the bathroom door my nan's voice floated back from the foot of the stairs.

'And don't think you're going to sit and stew in that bath all morning. If you're not done in five minutes, lady, I'll come and fetch you out myself.'

I rolled my eyes. And then I shouted back, 'Oh yeah? No offence, Nan, but how are you going to manage that exactly?'

'Easy peasy,' shouted my nan. 'I've taken the lock off the bathroom door.'

And, without even needing to check, I straight away knew that she had. Because that's another perfect example of what my nan is like. She's the sort of person who'll go to any amount of trouble just to make my life difficult. There's no doubt about it – my nan is hardcore.

And I realize now that this is exactly why my mum asked her to come and live with us.

Shaking my head at the total unfairness of it all, I kicked open the lockless bathroom door and started the water running in the basin.

Ronni Runnacles @ronneee_r

I live in a house full of ninjas.

It's not like other people's houses.

There's always somebody shouting or crying or farting or burping or cracking their knuckles or clicking their jaw or bum-bumping down the stairs or playing the armpit accordion or pretending to be Lionel Messi or Lord Voldemort or Usain Bolt. Or a ninja.

But when I finally made it down to breakfast yesterday morning, the whole house was quiet. If I'd pressed an ear to the wall, I'd probably have heard a big sigh of relief.

There were signs of my four little brothers everywhere. It looked like we'd been burgled. To be honest though, this is how our house usually looks. As I pushed open the kitchen door, I nearly went flying on half a pack of trading cards that had been left – like a booby trap – on the laminate floor. The cards were pictures of fat orange wrestlers with tattoos and handlebar moustaches. But, for all I cared, they might as well have looked like this:

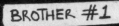
BROTHER #1

NAME: RYAN
AGE: 11
SPECIAL SKILLS:
TOXIC ODOURS

BROTHER #2

NAME: JACK
AGE: 7
SPECIAL SKILLS:
BREAKING THINGS

BROTHER #3

NAME: JOE
AGE: 5
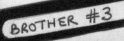
SPECIAL SKILLS:
SHOUTING REALLY
LOUDLY

BROTHER #4

NAME: HARRISON
AGE: 14 MONTHS
SPECIAL SKILLS:
NOT YET KNOWN

Four little brothers is **a lot** of little brothers. And even in those rare moments when our house is quiet you can never really relax, because you're always wondering where the chaos is going to come from next.

'Cute' Ryan had gone to school and forgotten his muddy football boots. They were festering – like a smelly reminder of his smelly existence – inside a smelly carrier bag on the kitchen worktop.

Jack – who trashes everything – had obviously tried to sneak his Nerf gun out of the house again. It had been tugged out of his hands – probably by my nan – and placed out of his reach on top of one of the kitchen cabinets.

Joe the Five-year-old Foghorn won't eat anything – including breakfast cereal – unless it comes with a dollop of tomato ketchup. There were sticky red blobs all over the breakfast table. There were quite a lot of those blobs on the floor as well.

And my smallest brother, Harrison, was busy redecorating the walls with porridge. He's the only one of my brothers who doesn't annoy me. This is because his

Annoying Boy Habits haven't developed yet. But it's only a matter of time.

Just a couple of months ago, my whole family went out to a posh cafe on the seafront and ate sandwiches and cake. It was to celebrate Harrison's first birthday. Everything seemed totally normal then.

But yesterday he was sitting in his high chair in our unposh kitchen and waving his spoon above his head. My mum was doing her best to persuade him to put the spoon in his mouth. She was smiling. It was such a rare sight that I had to do a double take to make sure I hadn't imagined it. And then when I saw that I hadn't and that she was actually smiling, I smiled too.

My mum glanced up, saw me and immediately stopped smiling. Then she looked back down at Harrison and said quietly, 'You're going to be late for school. Like you are every single flipping morning. You give me the pip, Ronni, you really do.'

My smile fell off my face. I picked up a box of cereal from the table, scooped up a handful of whatever was inside and shoved it in my mouth. After a bit of crunching, I nodded at Brother Number Four and said,

'Don't say *flipping* in front of Harrison.'

Harrison Harvey Runnacles beamed at me, said, 'Ron, Ron, Ron,' and lobbed another spoonful of porridge at the wall.

'Hiya, Harrison,' I said. And then I pulled back my ears and stuck my tongue out at him. Harrison shrieked with delight, clapped his hands and threw his spoon on to the floor.

My mum said, 'Don't wind him up.'

I looked at her. 'Hello? How am I winding him up? I was only saying hello.'

My mum didn't look at me. She picked up Harrison's spoon, reached for a cloth and wiped the porridge off the wall.

And then she said . . .

'You drive me . . . around . . .
the flipping . . . bend! You've
lazed about in that bed
every single morning for the
past month and waited for
someone to practically tip
you out of it. And then you
come straight down here and
wind the baby up! And don't
tell me what I can and *cannot*
say, Veronica Runnacles!
You're fourteen years old and
I'm thirty-eight! And I can
tell you now, I'd be saying a
helluva lot more than *flipping*
if Harrison wasn't sat here
between us – yes I *flipping
well would*!'

She said all of this without even looking at me once.

Taking another spoon from the kitchen drawer, my mum scraped a bit of escaped porridge from Harrison's chin and shovelled it back into his mouth. Harrison was making happy quacking noises like a happy duck. For one second I actually felt jealous. And then I shook my head, put on my tough face and said, 'Why are you having such a go at *me*?'

And finally my mum looked at me. But to be honest, I wish she hadn't. She had a face like a flat tyre.

I rolled my eyes to the ceiling and wished I was back in bed.

'I just . . . don't . . . understand you,' said my mum. 'You know how hard it is for me at the moment –'

I did a great big noisy sigh and rolled my eyes again.

'. . . It's hard for all of us,' she continued. 'But your brothers are coping OK. *They* get themselves out of bed and ready for school every morning and that's more than you can do! And they're younger than you are. They show you up, they really do.'

'Oh do they?' I said. 'Whoop!' And then I nodded at my mum, who was still wearing her pyjamas and a furry pink dressing gown, and said, 'It's a bit rich, isn't it? You talking to me about getting up and getting ready on time.'

'Yes, but I haven't got my GCSEs next year,' said my mum.

'Oh, big whoop,' I said. Harrison's face clouded over. I adjusted my attitude and quickly added, 'I need my sleep. I really do. It's not my fault if it takes me ages to wake up.'

My mum pulled a face. 'You managed to wake up pretty sharpish the other morning, didn't you? When they were doing those talent-show auditions. You didn't need your sleep then.'

Instantly, I felt a wave of shame and quickly looked at the floor. I didn't want to be reminded of this. The other week, me, Flooky and Kelly Bugg had got up at four in the morning so that we could get the train to London with Flooky's dad, who is Dutch. And then we had to wait in a queue for seven hours so that we could stand on a stage and sing twenty-six seconds of 'Pokerface' to a booing audience. And then Piers Morgan told us we were rubbish.

'And your schoolwork is going down the pan,' said my mum, who was clearly on a massive demolition roll. 'You used to be no trouble at all and now you're letting everything slide.'

'Oh yeah?' I slammed down the box of cereal. 'How would you even know that? You haven't got a clue what's going on in my life.'

My mum closed her eyes for a second and took a long deep breath. And then she opened them up again and ran the fingers of one hand through her hair. I noticed she was going grey where the dye had washed out. I suddenly felt bad.

My mum said, 'If you mess up school, you won't get any GCSEs. And if you don't get any GCSEs, you won't get into college. And if you don't go to college, how on earth do you think you're ever going to get a job?'

I looked down at the floor again. 'I dunno,' I said. It was the truth at least. Dobby – my careers teacher – once told us that the best jobs go to the candidates who stand out from the rest of the pack. I've never been someone who stands out from the pack. Until a month ago, I'm not even sure the teachers knew I existed.

They do now. But not in a good way.

I picked up the cereal box again and shoved another handful of dry stuff into my mouth.

'And I am interested in what you're up to,' said my mum. 'You might not think it, Ronni, but I am. How did you get on with that homework you had for *Black Beauty*?'

I froze.

My mum said, 'It was *Black Beauty*, wasn't it?'

My mouth was full of soggy cereal flakes so it was a few seconds before I could answer. Maybe that was a good thing. Slowly, I finished my mouthful and then I quietly said, 'We're not doing *Black Beauty*. We're doing *Alice in Wonderland*. And . . .'

Harrison squealed and began banging his new spoon against his tray. My mum put her mouth right up against his ear and started whispering to him.

'. . . Mrs Booley gave me an A* and a house point. She reckons it's the best bit of homework she's ever read.'

And then I just stopped. Because my mum had stopped listening. And it wasn't even true anyway.

The kitchen door opened and my nan appeared. She blew a kiss at Harrison and then gave me and my mum a frosty glare. 'Good morning, ladies,' she said. 'Or is it? I could hear you two belly-aching away at each other all the while I was doing my make-up. You've made me draw one of my eyebrows on wonky. I look like Ming the Merciless.'

I've got no idea who Ming the Merciless is, but she sounds quite rough so I'll take my nan's word for it.

My nan arched her scary eyebrow at my mum and said, 'I wasn't deliberately listening, but your volumes were up. Ronni was dead right when she said you shouldn't be wearing your pyjamas all day.'

Whoop, I thought. *Someone is actually listening to me!*

Then my nan turned her eyebrow towards me and said, 'And you, lady, get your gear together. I'm driving you to school.'

'I haven't finished my breakfast,' I said.

'See,' said my mum. 'She's impossible!'

'Hey,' said Ming the Merciless. 'Cut it out! The pair of you.' She looked back at me and said, 'If you wanted breakfast, lady, you should've got up earlier. So stop grizzling and get a shifty on. The Suzuki Swift is waiting.'

And all of a sudden I felt as if I'd just glugged down a billion energy drinks. Because there wasn't a single other thing my nan could have said to get me moving faster. Her driving totally gives me the willies.

'It's OK,' I said. 'I'll walk.'

'No you won't,' said my nan. 'You're late enough as it is. And it's raining like the apocalypse out there. I'm taking you. So either thank me or keep your trap shut.'

Harrison thinks my nan is hysterical. He clapped his hands together again and laughed. Then he chucked his second spoon on to the floor, dipped his hand into his porridge and lobbed a sticky missile straight at my nan's Golddigga tracksuit top. My nan laughed and said, 'Ooh, you're a cheeky one, aren't you?'

I laughed too. It totally lightened the atmosphere. For a second, our family actually felt normal.

But then my mum said, 'For God's sake, Ronni, I told you not to wind him up. You're just encouraging him.'

My jaw flopped open. 'I don't believe this! I haven't even done anything!'

'Come on, Ronni,' said my nan. 'Time to leave.'

'Gladly,' I said, and without bothering to say bye I

stormed out into the hallway to get my school bag. My eyes were stinging. Throwing open the front door, I stepped out and said, 'No wonder Dad wants a divorce. I'd divorce you too if I could. The whole flipping lot of you. Because I can't breathe in this situation.'

I knew it was a terrible thing to say, but I said it anyway. And it didn't really matter much because there wasn't a person in the entire world who was listening.

Ronni Runnacles @ronneee_r
Strictly speaking, this isn't
the worst town in the world.
#itjustfeelslikeitsometimes

But there's a lot more to my town than just a load of scruffy ships and office blocks.

There's a north beach and a south beach and a High Road East and a High Road West and shops and a boating lake and a pier and a promenade and a leisure centre and cafes and a cinema and a pool hall and ice-cream kiosks and tea rooms and amusement arcades and candy-floss huts and rows upon rows of big wooden tubs crammed full with nodding flowers. There's even an ancient fort on the sand dunes that stops us being invaded by France. And how many other places can say they've got one of those?

I always thought this stuff was cool. I really did. When all you've ever known is the friendly shout of seagulls overhead and the familiar smell of salt in the air and the fresh touch of the North Sea breeze against your face, you think that you'll want to hear and smell and feel these things forever. But one morning last month I woke up and everything was different. And after that I thought the whole place sucked like a Dyson and I wished I was somewhere else.

And I began to ask myself these three questions:

1. What's the point of having shops if there isn't an Apple store or a Hollister?

2. What's the point of a beach if it's covered in stones?

3. Who **actually** cares about old forts?

Questions like these are difficult and dangerous. There are no easy answers and if you spend too much time thinking about them you quickly start to feel let down. And, mostly, it's your mum and dad that you feel let down by. Because everything that's wrong is their fault. *They* are the ones who have forced you to live in Crapville instead of somewhere better – like New York or Hollywood.

And yesterday morning I was so wound up by all of this stuff that I was even annoyed with my nan. And, maybe, that explains why I was in such a filthy evil stinker of a mood when she reversed her car out of its parking space and roared away in the direction of my school.

You can spot my nan's car a mile off. It's a bright yellow Suzuki Swift with a special-edition shiny red roof. It looks like a slice of Edam and she drives it like she's a boy racer. But the worst thing about her car is the sticker in the back window. It says this:

HONK
IF YOU LIKE WHAT YOU SEE!

And whenever anyone honks – which happens more than it should – my nan always does a double honk back.

So I slunk down in the passenger seat of my nan's three-door cheesemobile and – for a second or two – I was so shocked by **the sheer unfairness of everything** that I couldn't even move. But then I sat up, fiddled with my seat belt, leaned forward, flicked the blowers on and off again and turned up the radio. The voice of some random old woman grumbled out of the speakers:

So I told him the country was going to the dogs and that's when he called me a silly old stick. He came crawling round my house later to apologize but only because the TV people were there. What kind of prime minister is that?

I retuned the radio to Meltdown FM and flumped back down in my seat.

My nan screeched round the corner at the end of our road and said, 'Hey, lady, I want it left on Radio 4. It's interesting.'

'Oh, *what*?' I looked at my nan in disbelief. 'Are you serious?'

Without taking her eyes off the road, my nan said, 'Can ducks swim?' And then – before I could even answer – she said, 'And sit up properly. If I were to brake sharpish, that seat belt would slice your head off.'

'For flip's sake,' I muttered. But, not wanting my day to get any worse, I obeyed both orders.

Back on Radio Bore, the random old lady was grumbling to a close. She whinged on for a few seconds longer and then the presenter thanked her and said:

And next, we move to a man who has devoted the last twelve years of his life to sugar-beet research. Dr Colin Gubbins of Wacton in north Norfolk has been conducting experiments to help British farmers produce pest-resistant crops. Dr Gubbins, thank you for joining us . . .

I sighed, shook my head and stared out at a world of rainy pavements and wheelie bins.

'Whoop,' I whispered.

Pushing my forehead against the side window, I lowered my eyelids and watched fat blobs of rain race each other across the other side of the glass. Raindrops look very different this close up. They look a lot more complicated. In fact, I could see tiny black wheelie bins being bent into weird shapes inside every single one of them.

Quickly, I shut my eyes to stop myself from going boss-eyed and then I opened them again and pushed my nose against the glass too. The wheelie bins were still there – but so was something else.

Inside the fattest raindrop, I saw a face.

I blinked and had another look. The face was still there. And now I could see that it wasn't just any old face – it was my face. And, as I watched, the raindrop grew and grew until I could see my neck and my shoulders and my whole body and everything around me as well.

Honestly, it's true. I actually saw a vision of myself inside a bubble of rainwater zooming across the side window of my nan's Suzuki Swift.

Or I think I did.

But, either way, it wasn't me as everyone else sees me – it was me as *I* sometimes see me. And I was sitting in a chauffeur-driven limo and sipping bubbly from a long-stemmed crystal glass while being whisked in comfort through the stylish streets and fashionable avenues of New York City.

My nan swerved to avoid a pigeon.

The raindrop splattered against the rim of the window and the vision of me in the limo disappeared. I fixed my eyes on another racing raindrop and imagined a different scenario. This time, I was standing on another stage at another festival in front of yet another sea of adoring fans . . .

I closed my eyes so that I could tune in properly, but instead of cheers and shouts and screams of applause all I could hear was a voice saying:

 I'm extremely excited because I'm very close to finding a way of extracting the syrup from the centrifuge without the flea beetle shot-holing the sugar-beet's vital development.

This wasn't right. I opened my eyes again, slid back down in my seat and went back to staring at wheelie bins.

We pulled up sharp at a set of traffic lights and, behind us, a car honked.

My nan said, 'Who is it?'

I twisted round in my seat and said, 'I dunno. It's some bloke in a blue van.'

My nan leaned forward to check out the honker in her rear-view mirror. Then she chuckled and said, 'It's Bouncy Castle Ken from my computer class. Pity. He's not really my cup of tea.' But she still waved and did the double honk back.

And even though I was in a proper evil stinker of a mood, I almost laughed. My nan might be a lock-stealing nightmare to live with but she cracks me up. Sometimes, she cracks me up so much that I have to talk about her on Twitter. Like this:

 **Ronni Runnacles** @ronneee_r
My nan skyplussed a Dizzee Rascal gig because she thought he was a jazz trumpeter. #fail

Or this:

 **Ronni Runnacles** @ronneee_r
My nan is currently reading #50shadesofgrey behind the argos catalogue. #yuck

On impulse, I reached into my coat pocket for my phone. It wasn't there. I'd left it in my bed. I shut my eyes and muttered, 'Oh, that's flipping brilliant!'

My nan said, 'Oh, I wouldn't say Ken's brilliant, but he did help me get the winning bid on a New York Fire Department Calendar on the eBays. Even so, I still wouldn't want him to squeeze my toothpaste.'

I stopped thinking about my forgotten phone and this time I did actually laugh.

My nan said, 'You're as pretty as a picture when you smile, Ronni. You should do it more often, lady. You've got nothing to lose. A smile is something you can't give away. It always comes back to you.' And then she turned her head and smiled at me.

And – in spite of everything – I smiled back. I couldn't help it. I was starting to feel a lot more relaxed.

Then my nan said, 'Ronni, I know we've been through all this before and I know you don't want to talk about it and you don't want your friends to hear about it and you don't want us to say anything to your school – but it's never good bottling stuff up. And if you decide you ever do want to talk to someone about what's happened with your dad, you can always talk to me. You know that, don't you?'

And instantly I tensed up again.

'Yeah, but I don't,' I said.

My nan shook her head and muttered, 'Selfish bloody man!' And then she said, 'Well, sometimes it helps to . . . Oh . . . hang about . . .'

The traffic lights turned to amber and then green. My nan released the handbrake and sent us roaring forward. The way she drives, you'd think she was playing Burnout on the pier. I crossed my fingers and desperately hoped she'd let the subject drop.

My nan said, 'I just think—'

'Yeah, but I don't care,' I said really quickly. 'And I don't want to have this conversation. So can we just listen to the radio, please?' And I leaned forward and turned the volume right up.

'Fair enough,' said my nan. 'But the offer is always there. Sometimes, a natter with your nan is just what you need when everything's gone downside up.'

And I knew she was only being nice, but it really wasn't helping. Because up until my dad left I never ever dreamed

54

that we might one day need that type of natter.

My nan turned the volume down to a more comfortable level, nodded her head at the window and said, 'You get a smashing view of the docks from along here.'

I didn't say anything.

My nan nodded her head again and said, 'Good to see that flame's still burning.'

I shifted my eyes so that I could see the flame she was talking about. Through the gaps between the houses, I could see a backdrop of ships and cranes and metal containers. And leaping out from all this greyness was the orange flame I'd looked for earlier from my bedroom window and which I look for every morning from my bedroom window.

My nan said, 'If that ever went out, we'd all explode. BOOM.'

I still didn't say anything. And, after that, my nan didn't either.

Several silent centuries later, we pulled up at the school gates. My nan switched off the engine, folded her arms and said, 'Right, lady, get yourself over to that reception and sign in. If you get a shift on, you should catch the end of your first lesson.'

'Whatever,' I mumbled. Then I leaned down, grabbed hold of my bag and opened the car door.

My nan said, 'Oh, and Ronni?'

'What?'

My nan said, 'You do know you'll always be my favourite granddaughter, don't you?'

I paused. And then I turned back to her with a smile and said, 'See you later, Nan.' And, waving goodbye, I headed off towards my school gates feeling miles better than I had done all morning. Because, even though I'm my nan's only granddaughter, it's still a nice thing to hear her say. And when my nan uses a word like *always*, I'm pretty sure she actually means it.

I hurried off through the rain in the direction of reception. Suddenly, it seemed really important to try to get my day back on track and get my name in the late book as quickly as I could so that I could catch the end of my first lesson – just like my favourite nan wanted.

But then I spotted Stuart Bolan in the bike shed and stopped.

He was sat on the saddle of someone else's parked mountain bike and eating an ice cream. I know it wasn't *his* bike because – just as I looked over to him – he tipped his head back, shook the remaining ice cream into his mouth and then rammed the cone on to the end of one of the bike's handlebars. And then he sparked up a fag.

Everyone fancies Stuart Bolan. You only have to look at him to understand why.

Stuart Bolan is one of those people who wears school uniform and at the same time manages to stick two fingers up at it. Instead of regulation black trousers, he wears greying skinny jeans and somehow gets let off the hook. Instead of his regulation white school shirt, he mostly wears his regulation white PE polo. The lapel of his bottle-green blazer is practically hidden by badges and the knot in his tie is fatter than any other tie-knot I've ever seen. I honestly don't know how he does it. Anyone else would be in detention forever.

Everyone fancies Stuart Bolan because he's cooler than Pope John Cool II.

So I changed direction, crossed the yard, ducked my head under the low roof of the cycle shed and said, 'Hi, Stu, what's up?'

Stuart flicked his bleached fringe out of his face and tilted his head back to look at me. Then he said, 'Oh, it's you.'

Up until a month ago, I don't think Stuart Bolan really knew I existed. But then he started seeing me in late detentions and knew that I definitely did. I can't honestly say that he seemed excited about it though.

Not totally sure how to respond, I shrugged my shoulders and said, 'Oh, so it is!'

Stuart raised his hand to show me his cigarette. 'I was having a smoke.'

And because I wasn't totally sure how to respond to this either, I just shrugged my shoulders again and said, 'Whoop!'

Stuart Bolan stared at me. Then he shook his head very slowly and said, 'Zing!'

Zing?

I leaned against a wooden post and tried to act cool. It wasn't easy. In fact, I was already finding Stuart Bolan way too cool for comfort. But it still beat being in maths.

Stuart patted his pockets, located a plastic lighter and sparked up the cigarette he'd only lit a few moments earlier. Then he took a big slow drag. And then he started coughing.

I wasn't quite sure what to do with myself. So I just stood there.

When he'd finished coughing, Stuart flicked his fringe

out of his face again and said, 'Did I just see you get out of a really smart little Suzuki Swift? Three doors? Chrome alloys? Personal specification paintwork?'

This was better. I nodded. 'Yeah. That's my nan's car. She got it from a garage in Ipswich.'

Stuart Bolan kept on coolly staring at me from underneath his cool fringe. Then he opened his mouth up into an O shape, blew out a smoke ring and said, 'That . . . is . . . fas-cin-a-ting.'

And something about the way he said it gave me this niggling feeling that he didn't actually mean it and that I wasn't being fas-cin-a-ting at all. I was being really, **really** *bor-ing*. And it was a bad feeling to have because this wasn't my first conversation fail of the day. And it wasn't even half-past nine yet.

So I dug deeper, opened up my mouth again and made a bigger effort to be interesting . . .

Well, I'll tell you something else about my nan. She hasn't been the same since that time the prime minister called her a daft old bag on the news. He only said it quietly but he'd forgotten to take his microphone off. And then he came round our house with a film crew and said sorry. Because my nan lives with us, you see. She has done since my dad went away. And I don't know what the prime minister said exactly but it must have been one helluva grovel because my nan was in all the newspapers for days. She even got asked to be a guest on *The One Show* but she had to turn it down because it clashed with her OAP computer class. But I actually feel slightly sorry for the prime minister because my nan is a daft old bag sometimes. Especially first thing in the mornings. But, then again, the prime minister *was* stupid. He shouldn't have rocked up uninvited to my nan's computer club and started asking everyone how they wanted the country to be run. Not when the bidding was just about to finish on a signed calendar of the New York Fire Department wearing nothing but their undies. That's what you call really pants timing!

And then I clamped my gob shut and wished I could take back that really random bit about the firemen.

Stuart Bolan's mouth curled into a grin. 'Yeah, right? I don't remember hearing anything about that.'

My face went hot and I wished I could take it all back. But then he said, 'Mind you, I never bother with the news. It's well boring.'

My face cooled down and I felt OK again. In fact, I probably felt quite a bit better than OK. Because the truth was that I was on my own in the bike shed with Stuart Bolan – who everybody fancies – and me and him were having a friendly personal conversation. And we both should have been in maths.

Stuart said, 'So where's your dad then?'

The OK feeling evaporated.

Stuart said, 'You just said your nan lives with you because your dad went away. So where is he?'

'Oh,' I said, and I frowned. 'Did I say that?' My face had gone hot again. Really hot.

'Yeah,' said Stuart. 'You did.'

And suddenly I'd had enough of this personal conversation. It was too personal. Way too personal. In fact, it was making me wish I'd just gone straight to maths. For a horrible second, I could feel my throat closing up and my eyes melting – but then I switched reality off, opened up my mouth and said . . .

> My dad is away at the moment. In north Norfolk. He's a scientist and he does all this really important research to help farmers produce pest-resistant crops of sugar beet.

It was the first thing I could think of.

Stuart Bolan raised his eyebrows. And then he took another drag on his cigarette, stumped it out on the crossbar of his borrowed bike and carefully put it into his blazer pocket. To be totally honest, I don't like cigarettes. They make people smell manky. But, to be fair, Stuart Bolan didn't look manky. He looked well buff.

And I guess I must have forgotten which channel I was tuned into because I opened my mouth and said, 'Do you want to come to the pier with me on Saturday? I'm really good at playing Burnout.'

I actually said it out loud. It wasn't in my head or anything.

Stuart Bolan smiled, pedalled backwards and said, 'Are you asking me out?'

So I smiled back and said, 'If you like.'

And Stuart ran one hand through his hair, pedalled backwards some more and said, 'Dream on, Cake Girl. Last I heard, even the tide wouldn't take you out!'

And then he said, 'Joke,' and started laughing.

For a second, I just stood there confused.

Cake Girl?

A picture of the fight in the food-tech room popped into my head. I could see myself hurling sponge mix at Sadie Slowgrove's head – just as if I was some kind of Nigella ninja. For the millionth time that morning, I felt my cheeks go hot. And then – because it would have been really massively awkward otherwise – I just shrugged my shoulders and laughed too. Sometimes it's the easiest thing to do.

And maybe I'd have stood there for the rest of my life going ha ha ha over something that wasn't even funny had I not been distracted by a very loud cough. And wherever that cough had come from, it definitely hadn't come from me. And, even though he'd been smoking like a barbecue, it hadn't come from Stuart Bolan either.

So we both looked around.

Half hidden behind a barricade of spokes was Yuri

Maximovich Krolik. He's one of the foreign kids. Even though he's in the same class as me for maths and English, I'd never given him a second glance until that precise moment. To be fair, he's quite easy to miss. He's quite tall and quite thin and quite quiet and quite ordinary-looking. You can't miss him completely though – because Yuri Maximovich Krolik is also quite odd.

And, in case you're wondering, he happens to be Russian. That's why he's got a name like Yuri Maximovich Krolik. Nobody ever calls him that though. Everybody calls him Spaceman.

He was sitting on the bare ground of the bike shed and reading a book. When he saw us looking at him, he lowered his book and said, 'Hello.'

Stuart Bolan's eyebrows rose in surprise and then he said, 'What are you doing here, Spaceman?'

Yuri pushed a strand of mousy hair away from his grey eyes and said, 'Yes. I read intense Russian novel. But please not to call me Spaceman. My name is Yuri Maximovich Krolik.'

Yuri Maximovich Krolik's English isn't too hot.

Stuart Bolan said, 'Mate, you are SO random,' and started laughing all over again.

This is a fairly standard reaction. Most people think Yuri is a bit random. And it's not because he's the only Russian boy in our school. It's more to do with the fact that he walks around with biros tucked behind his ears. And the handles of his sports bag wrapped round his forehead. And because he bunks off lessons and sits in the corner of the bike shed reading intense Russian novels when he should be in maths with me and Stuart Bolan and everyone else.

Yuri Maximovich Krolik didn't seem to care that he was being laughed at. In fact, he hardly seemed to notice it. He was too busy staring at me with a great big frown on his face. I don't like being frowned at. So I frowned back at him and said, 'What's your problem?'

Yuri took a long time to think about this. Then – instead of answering – he jerked his head at Stuart and said, 'Yes. But why you laugh with him?'

I looked across at Stuart and made a face that said *What is he on?* And then I looked back at Yuri and said, 'What d'you mean?'

'I hear you as I read my book. You laugh with him. Why?'

'I don't flipping know,' I said. 'Do I need a reason?'

Yuri's frown deepened and he seemed to think about it a bit

more. Then he said, 'Yes, well, you are idiot because I hear you as I read my book and you were laughing at joke which is not funny.'

My frown deepened too. And then, amazed, I said, 'Did I just hear that right? Did you just call me an idiot?'

'Yes,' said Yuri.

Stuart Bolan rang the bell on his burgled bike and said, 'Oh, mate, just keep talking. You're flipping priceless!' And he started laughing even louder.

And because it was such a completely weird conversation, I started laughing too. A bit. And then I said, 'Well, thanks a lot, Spaceman!'

Yuri nodded stiffly at me. 'Yes. It is OK. You are welcome. But please not to call me Spaceman. My name is Yuri Maximovich Krolik.' And he stood up, wrapped the handles of his bag round his forehead and stomped off through the rain to the maths block.

By now, Stuart Bolan was laughing so much that he couldn't sit up straight. He was slumped all over the bike's handlebars and looked as if he was suffering from some kind of serious laughter-shock.

I was still laughing too. A bit.

Stuart finally stopped laughing. He lifted his head up, shook it very slowly and said, 'That kid is such a freak!'

And even though it was a massive relief to know that Stuart Bolan wasn't laughing at me this time, I felt more uncomfortable than ever.

Because freak is a pretty harsh word.

Even when you're using it to describe someone who hangs his bag off his head.

Ronni Runnacles @ronneee_r

I hate getting up.

I won't lie to you. I've never been what you could call an early bird. I've always liked being in bed. But about a month ago I lost the battle with my pillow and started sleeping right through my morning alarm. And the times when I did hear it, I just pulled the duvet over my head and pretended I hadn't. And when my mum yelled up at me from the bottom of the stairs I closed my ears and didn't move. And I also closed my ears when my brothers started yelling too.

But then my nan rocked up. She moved her stuff into the front room, set up shop on the sofa bed and never left. And that made my mornings more complicated.

But even my nan can't always get me to shift. So I started having to write my name in the Late Book. Strictly speaking, it's not even a book. It's a fat, tatty file that lives on the desk of the Student Reception. To put it in the most basic terms possible, the Late Book is a big long list of all the duvet lovers and morning haters and slow-moving people in my school. My name is on that list twelve times.

Twelve times in one month. I think that's some sort of a record.

My brother Ryan has **never** had his name in the Late Book. Not once. Not even with all the stuff that's been going on at home. Until yesterday, this annoyed me so much that I got traumatized just thinking about it. But now I've thought about it some more and I think he deserves a bit of respect. I really seriously do.

After I left Stuart Bolan laughing his cockles off in the bike shed, I wasn't thinking about any of this though. The one thing on my mind was the question of how to get my name into the Late Book without Mr Scrunton seeing me put it there. Because whenever Scrunton spots anyone signing in late he always comes skittering out of his little glass-fronted office to dish out a big dose of unnecessary ear ache. That man is a human earwig.

And, to make matters **even** worse, it turned out that Mr Scrunton wasn't my only problem. Sitting behind the desk in Student Reception and proudly wearing the Student Receptionist sash was Sadie Slowgrove. It actually made me wish that I'd just done myself a favour and got up when the alarm went off.

Sadie Slowgrove looked at me and silently pushed the Late Book and Late Pen across the desk. And then she took out a bendy nail file from the pocket of her blazer and started grinding her claws down.

Even though I was worried about being caught by Scrunton, I took a scrunchy out of my pocket and – in deliberate slow motion – I threaded my hair into a ponytail. I knew it was one heckuva stupid moment to be doing that, but I did it anyway. And then I calmly opened up the Late Book, picked up the Late Pen and began to write my name on the correct Late Page. I hadn't even finished the V of Veronica when I heard the door of the glass office open. And then I heard a voice say, 'Sneaking in late, are we?'

Sadie Slowgrove dropped her bendy nail file back into her pocket and sat up straight.

My heart plummeted. I sighed, scrawled down the rest of my name and turned round to face the music.

Mr Scrunton was standing eerily still with his arms folded and his shoulders hunched up around his neck. Mostly, he wears horrible beige suits but this time he was wearing a horrible black one. It suited him. He looked like a big black beetle. Or – like I said earlier – an earwig.

Mr Scrunton said, 'Well, well, well . . . If it isn't Miss Runnacles again! Good of you to join us.'

I should just explain something. Mr Scrunton is **not** the Headteacher. And he's **not** the Deputy Headteacher. He's **not** a Head of Year. Or an Assistant Head of Year. Or a Head of Department. Or a Head of House. This doesn't stop him being bossy though. Because, in Mr Scrunton's head, he's **way more important** than any of them. In Mr Scrunton's head, he's the **King of the Earwigs**.

In real life, he's the School Reception Manager.

So I stood there in front of the King of the Earwigs, puffed out my cheeks and waited for him to say something else. So did Sadie Slowgrove. I suppose the big difference was that she was enjoying herself.

'It's Friday,' said Mr Scrunton.

Whoop whoop, I thought. *Well done.*

'And you're **late**. Very **late**. You've completely missed Lesson One. That was maths, wasn't it? A useful subject. Numbers will never go out of fashion. And, if my own maths is correct, you've already been **late** three times this week.

Or is it four times? Just recently, you're late so often, Miss Runnacles, I'm losing count. In fact, you're becoming such a regular star of the Late Book that we may have to invest in another volume just for you. And what makes you late today?'

Every time he said the word late, I caught a breath-bomb of stale coffee.

Sadie Slowgrove folded her arms and smiled. It was the happiest I'd seen her look for a whole month. If I'd had a bowl of Victoria-sponge cake mix handy I might have hurled it at her.

Mr Scrunton said, 'Please do explain. I'm all ears.'

No you're not, I thought. *You're a douchebag.* I didn't say this though. What I actually said was, 'I'd prefer to discuss it with my form tutor if you don't mind. It's personal. I've got some problems at home.'

Sadie Slowgrove's smile flickered. And then it disappeared. Her face went a bit pink and she looked down at her hands and started staring at her nails.

Mr Scrunton looked annoyed, but he didn't push it. Instead, he folded his arms and said, 'Do you know who Admiral Nelson is?'

I stared at him. *What kind of randomness is this?*

After a puzzled pause, I said, 'Yes.' And then I added, 'Sort of.' And then I added, 'No.'

Mr Scrunton stopped looking annoyed and started looking smug. 'Admiral Nelson happens to be the gentleman who stands on top of the column in Trafalgar Square.' He paused and then added, 'That's in *London*.'

'I do *know* that,' I said.

Mr Scrunton ignored me and carried on. 'And Nelson once remarked, *I have always been a quarter of an hour ahead of my time and it has made a man of me.* Perhaps you could learn something from those wise words, Miss Runnacles.'

Even Sadie Slowgrove was beginning to look bored.

I frowned. 'Yeah, but I don't want to be a man, do I? And, anyway, my nan always reckons *better late than never*.'

Mr Scrunton's nose wrinkled up as if he'd just caught a whiff of his own breath. And then he said, 'How wise. But arriving on time is hardly rocket science. It's just a matter of waking up when you're supposed to wake up and generally being a bit better organized.'

I can't be sure, but I think Sadie Slowgrove was starting to look ever so slightly sorry for me. That's the magic effect that

Scrunton has on people. He unites everyone against him. It's a kind of unlucky gift, I suppose.

But then Sadie Slowgrove must have remembered what the situation was between us because she began to glare at me again.

I took a slow deep breath. Looking Mr Scrunton right in the eye, I said, 'Do you mind if I go now, please? If I stand here and chat any longer, I'll be late for English as well.'

And even though I could tell he didn't like it **one little bit**, the King of the Earwigs **finally** stood aside and let me escape.

Ronni Runnacles @ronneee_r

Sticks and stones will break my bones but words will never hurt me. #yeahright

Believe that and you'll believe anything.

I sat very still in my seat and stared at the random George Clooney poster on the wall of the classroom. And then I looked down and stared at the question that Mrs Booley had written at the bottom of my English homework.

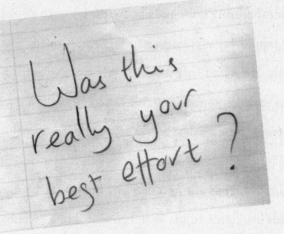

Was this really your best effort?

Six little words and a question mark. That was all. But together they felt like a giant slap in the face. I don't like getting bad marks in English. It's always been one of my best subjects. Up until a month ago anyway.

I stared at the scrawled pencil message for at least half a century and prickled all over. And then I sighed very noisily, lifted my head and looked my English teacher right in the eye. 'I don't think that's fair,' I said. 'I'm actually quite upset by that remark. I spent ages writing this.'

Mrs Booley parked a buttock on the edge of my desk and raised her eyebrows in exaggerated surprise. Then she tucked one edge of her grey bob behind her ear, put on the glasses hanging handily from an orange cord round her neck and said, 'Well, if that's really the case, Ronni, we need to get your processing skills and handwriting speeds re-examined.' She tapped my essay with her finger and added, 'But you can surely understand my concern? What you've written isn't more than three sentences long. We can hardly call that a character profile. I think we'd be better off calling it a tweet.'

I flinched. I don't know why exactly, but it never sounds natural when people as old as Mrs Booley start bandying about words like *tweet*. It just sounds wrong. For a second, it even got me wondering whether she'd been going to the exact same computer class as my nan and Bouncy Castle Ken. They had a session one evening called *Sixty-somethings Can Tweet Too*.

Mrs Booley said, 'I write more than that on my Palm Pixi.'

I flinched all over again. And then I put my elbows on the desk, leaned my head in my hands and said, 'So what are you saying?'

'I'm saying your work looks rushed,' said Mrs Booley. 'And I don't think you've been focusing anywhere near enough recently.' And then she pointed to the random poster on the wall and said, 'Do you think George Clooney conquered Hollywood without making a genuine effort?'

I shrugged. 'I dunno. Anyway, I had loads of other stuff to do.'

Mrs Booley instantly looked cheesed off. I rolled my eyes, slid down in my seat and wished I'd just stayed in the bike shed with Stuart Bolan.

Mrs Booley said, 'Oh I see. And what sort of *other stuff* did you have to do which was so much more important than your English homework?'

It wasn't an interesting question and it didn't have an interesting answer. I closed my eyes and switched to a more entertaining channel.

You really want to me to answer that?'

Mrs Booley said, 'Oh, I do. Absolutely. Please, Ronni! It would be a kindness. You'd be putting some sparkle back into my life.'

I could tell from the desperate look in her eyes that she was deadly serious and it was impossible not to feel sorry for her.

So I smiled gently and said, 'Well, let me see. Last weekend was completely impossible for homework because I was headlining on the Pyramid Stage at the Glastonbury Festival. And Monday and Tuesday were a no-no because of all the after-parties and interviews. And Wednesday was taken up with making a promo video, and yesterday we were in the recording studio throwing down a few tracks for the new album. So, actually, it's a miracle that I've even turned up for school today.'

Mrs Booley said, 'Ronni, don't close your eyes when I'm talking to you.'

I opened them, glared at my desk for a moment and then I just told her the truth. 'I had to babysit for my brothers. My mum's not feeling good at the moment and my nan lives with us, but she can't do everything.'

Mrs Booley frowned. I waited for her to have another go at me but she didn't. Instead, she parked her other buttock on my desk too, and – in a low voice – said, 'Is everything OK with you, Ronni?'

'Yeah,' I said.

Mrs Booley didn't move. She just kept on sitting there and staring at me. I didn't know where to look so I put my head down again and stared at my desk. On it, someone had written:

I'D GIVE MY RIGHT
ARM TO BE
AMBIDEXTROUS.

And even though it was the worst joke in the world, I smiled.

Mrs Booley said, 'Oh. Well, I can see you're finding this

conversation amusing.' And with that she lifted both buttocks off the desk, stood up and said, 'Mr Krolik, can you give everybody a copy of *Alice's Adventures in Wonderland*, please?' And then she glared at me over the top of her glasses and walked off.

I shut my eyes and sat very still for a second. When I opened them, I screwed my homework into a tight ball and threw it straight across the desk at George Clooney's face. Unfortunately, Kelly Bugg – who sits directly opposite me – chose just that same moment to stand up and adjust her tights. My homework bounced off Kelly's head and fell to the floor.

Kelly Bugg looked worried. 'No offence,' she said, 'but I take it you got another crap mark then.' And she stooped down, picked the ball of paper up and unscrunched it to see what Mrs Booley had written.

'Excuse me, that's private,' I said.

Kelly's face fell. 'No offence, Ronni. I was just interested.' And she re-scrunched it and chucked it back across the table at Flooky. Then she carried on de-wrinkling her tights and sat down again.

Flooky – who is Goal Attack in the school netball team –

caught my ball of homework neatly and hurled it as hard as she could across the classroom. It hit Yuri Maximovich Krolik square in the chest, but I don't know if he noticed because he was too busy balancing a stack of those *Alice's Adventures in Wonderland* books on his head.

Mrs Booley finished her tour of the classroom, glanced around and said, 'I asked you to hand out those reading books, Mr Krolik. Not wear them as a hat.'

Yuri tipped his head forward and let the books fall into his arms. Then he carefully restacked them so that all the covers were the same way round and all the spines were in line with the pencil he'd taken out from behind his ear. When he was satisfied that they were, he began to wander around the room plonking them down in front of people.

Flooky was watching him. She shook her head slowly and said, 'That kid is such a space cadet.' And then she turned her eyes to me and said, 'Not that I was deliberately listening – but why didn't you just tell The Booley that everything is not OK with you. Because it blatantly isn't.'

A big lump began to rise in my throat. 'It's none of her business,' I said. 'And, anyway, everything's fine. My nan's just staying with us until my mum cheers up, that's all. It's no big deal.'

Flooky and Kelly Bugg exchanged a glance.

I looked at them. 'What's that supposed to mean?'

Flooky and Kelly Bugg exchanged another glance. Finally, very quietly, Kelly Bugg said, 'No offence, Ronni, but we both know your dad has gone away. To be honest, everyone knows.'

Flooky said, 'Yeah. Your nan told her friend Shirley Gammon who told her friend Lesley Sweatbanks who told her friend Janice Beany who told my mum who told me.'

I kept on looking at them. They kept on looking back at me. I wondered how much else they knew. I wondered if they knew where my dad had gone away to and exactly who he'd gone there with.

The lump in my throat rose higher. With a big gulp, I swallowed it down. Then – before I'd even had a chance to check it with my brain – I opened up my gob and said, 'God, I hate living in this stupid town. Everyone is dead nosy. He's just working away, that's all. He's doing important stuff for the government.'

Flooky and Kelly Bugg exchanged yet another meaningful glance. This time, I think that even George Clooney was joining in.

Mrs Booley called over, 'Is everything OK in that corner?'

'Yeah,' I called back. And then I looked back at Flooky and Kelly and Clooney and hissed, 'Just stop thinking you know what you're talking about. Because you don't!' And I might have been on the brink of saying some other stuff too but the door of the classroom opened and made us all turn around.

It was Sadie Slowgrove. She said, 'Sorry I'm late. I was doing reception duty.'

I followed her with my eyes as she went to her seat. And then I rested my forehead on my fingertips and did some more hard swallowing. I felt sick. It was like I'd just developed mumps or something. As soon as I could trust my voice, I shook my head crossly and muttered, 'You two don't know anything. You don't understand. Nobody does.'

Kelly Bugg looked anxious. 'We're just really worried about you, Ronni. No offence, but if you keep getting crap marks you'll get moved down into a lower set.'

'Whoop,' I said.

Flooky looked annoyed. 'Don't expect us to sit by and watch you sink without saying something. If you're not careful, you'll be sitting in a room by yourself next year reading Topsy and Tim books.'

'Whoop,' I said.

Yuri Krolik plonked three copies of *Alice in Wonderland* on our table. Then he just stood there looking at us.

Flooky said, 'Yes? Can we do something for you?'

Yuri cleared his throat, looked right at me and said, 'This is intense book with hidden meaning. I can help you understand.'

Straight away, I said, 'I can understand it by myself, thank you.' For some reason, I was suddenly massively embarrassed.

Yuri shrugged and moved on to the next table.

Flooky shook her head slowly and said, 'What . . . the . . . heck . . . is he on?'

Kelly Bugg folded her arms. 'No offence, Ronni, but do you really want to be stuck in an English class with him next year?'

But I didn't get a chance to answer. Mrs Booley said, 'OK, class, can I have you all quiet now, please. I'm waiting . . . I'm waiting . . . I'm *still* waiting . . . Tamika, stop talking, please . . . Kelsey, stop talking . . . Yuri, take the book off your head . . . OK . . . Okayyy . . . And let's all turn to page seventy-eight. Now, before we continue, let's think about what we've read so far. This book may seem to be nothing more than a lot of fun and nonsense – but *is* it all nonsense? Or is there something much more meaningful going on just beneath the surface?'

The entire class was silent.

Mrs Booley peered at us hopefully over the tops of her glasses.

We all stared blankly back at her.

Mrs Booley said, 'Okayyy . . . let me ask you another question. Why does Alice follow the White Rabbit down the rabbit hole?'

Nobody spoke.

Mrs Booley looked around the class. And then she spotted me and smelt blood. 'Ronni,' she said, 'I'll start with you.'

I said, 'Oh, but—'

Mrs Booley said, 'No buts! George Clooney didn't win an Oscar for his role in *Syriana* by saying *but*.'

'Flipping heck,' I muttered. And then I frowned because I seriously didn't have a clue what to say. Why would anyone go down a rabbit hole?

Mrs Booley cupped her hand behind her ear and said, 'You'll have to speak up. I didn't catch that.'

Everyone was looking at me and waiting for me to answer. It made me feel really pressurized. Especially as I didn't have an answer. So in the end, I just pulled my tough face and said,

'How the heck should I know why she goes down a rabbit hole?'

I almost hoped Mrs Booley would send me straight out of the classroom and put me out of my misery. But instead of getting cross, she just took off her glasses and smiled patiently. Then she said, 'Oh, come on, Ronni, you're not trying. This isn't a difficult question. You must have some thoughts as to why Alice follows the White Rabbit.'

I shrugged helplessly. 'Because she's a sad idiot.'

A few people in the class laughed. I looked around at them and smiled. But then I spotted Yuri Maximovich Krolik and my smile faded. He'd tilted his head right back as far as his neck would allow and was balancing his open book flat on his face. And earlier – in the bike sheds – he'd called me an idiot!

My face went hot.

Mrs Booley said, 'Yes . . . well . . . Alice certainly behaves in a very strange way. But is her adventure purely nonsense or is Lewis Carroll trying to suggest something else? Does anyone else have any ideas?'

Yuri Krolik raised his hand and his head. The book fell from his face with a crash.

'Yes, Mr Krolik.'

'She is boring,' said Yuri.

Mrs Booley smiled. 'I think you mean bored, Yuri. And yes, I agree. Alice is bored. Of what?'

'Of real world,' said Yuri. 'She believes it is very boring place which limits her possibilities of leading exciting unboring life. And by following interesting rabbit person, she is actually escaping boring life and looking for adventures.'

Everyone turned to look at Yuri in astonishment. He cracked a couple of knuckles, scratched his elbow and added, 'And then Alice finds very small door inside very small rabbit hole so she has to drink very strange drink to turn herself very small. And then to make herself big again, she eats very strange cake. But now she is too big. And it feels very wrong. And this is *not* writer nonsense – this is deeply intense book highlighting stress and confusion of being teenager.' And then he picked his pencil up and started poking himself in the ear with it.

Mrs Booley looked impressed. I was impressed too. Yuri Maximovich Krolik might be a bit of a spaceman and his grasp of English might not be that hot, but he definitely knows a thing or two about books.

Mrs Booley said, 'Thank you, Yuri. Goodness gracious!

Responses like that put some sparkle back into my life! Yes. Mr Krolik is quite right. In the novel *Alice's Adventures in Wonderland* we have a central character who feels unfulfilled and bored by reality. So she seeks an alternative reality. And maybe the reason she is so bored is because she's finding the journey from childhood to adulthood very difficult.' Mrs Booley looked at me again and said, 'Do you still judge Alice so harshly, Ronni?'

I thought about it for a second but then I got bored and shrugged. 'Yeah. If she wants a more interesting life, she should do something sensible about it. Running off with a random rabbit is hardly going to help, is it?'

Mrs Booley was about to say something more but the door opened again. I looked around. So did everyone else. To my utter horror, I saw the face of Brother Number One – Ryan – peeping nervously into the classroom. He's in Year 7. I'm in Year 9. At school, our paths are not supposed to cross.

Ryan looked around, saw Mrs Booley at the front of the class and said, 'CanIgiveanotetomysisterplease?'

Hannah-Michelle Peach – who hasn't got a bad word to say about anybody – said, 'Ohmigod! That little boy is soooo gooooorrrrrrrgeous.'

Tamika Hardwick – who sits next to her and is a total bitch – said, 'Yeah. There's no way you'd ever think he was Ronni's brother, would you? What the hell happened there?'

'For God's sake, Tamika,' I said. 'Who rattled your cage?'

'That's enough, Ronni,' said Mrs Booley.

I said, 'But—'

'No buts,' said Mrs Booley. And then she looked at Ryan with the same sort of look you'd give to a Labradoodle puppy and said, 'Of course you can, dear, but be quick about it.'

Ryan put his head down, did a speed-walk over to where I was sitting and dropped a folded-up piece of paper into my lap. Then he turned around, put his head down again and did a speed-walk straight back across the room and out through the door.

I unfolded the note and stared at it.

Ronni, it has come to our attention that you have the most pathetic life on the planet.

From everyone else in the world.

I kept on staring at it.

Dimly, in the background somewhere, I heard a voice say, 'That's a big frown on your face, Ronni. Not bad news I hope.'

I flinched. It was Mrs Booley. She was making me flinch rather a lot this lesson. And she'd balanced a buttock on my desk again. I'd been so lost in my own thoughts that I hadn't even heard her crossing the room. I looked up in surprise. And then I said, 'I dunno. I haven't read it yet.'

Mrs Booley looked confused and scratched her head. Then she said, 'Well, you'd better read it.'

I nodded and stared down at the note again and this time I looked properly at the words which were written on it.

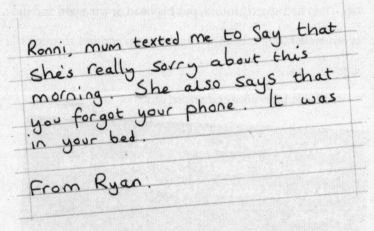

Ronni, mum texted me to say that she's really sorry about this morning. She also says that you forgot your phone. It was in your bed.

From Ryan.

I read it carefully. And then I read it again. And then I looked up at Mrs Booley and I actually smiled. 'No bad news.'

'Thank goodness for that.' Mrs Booley patted me on the arm, walked back to the front of the class and said, 'OK, Kelsey, start reading from the top of page seventy-eight. Everyone else follow along, please.'

So Kelsey started reading out loud from the top of page 78 and the heads of everyone in the class nodded forward over their books. And **my** head nodded forward too and I **really was trying** to do as Mrs Booley had asked because I suddenly wanted to know what was going to happen next to the weird messed-up girl in my book.

But I couldn't do it.

Because the TV set in my head was jammed on a **totally different channel.** Instead of following the words of *Alice in Wonderland*, all I could think about was Ronni Runaway filming her new video and dancing in a spotlight of sunshine next to a rabbit hole far far away.

Ronni Runnacles @ronneee_r

When I was 10, I wanted to be
Hermione Granger. #getreal

But then I changed my mind and decided I'd rather be Beyoncé instead.

Even at ten I knew this was a lot to hope for. Beyoncé is probably one of the most famous people on the planet. So I shifted my horizons a little and decided that I'd be better off being Beyonce's band mate, Kelly Rowland.

But after a while, I got a bit worried about this idea too. Kelly Rowland might not be Beyoncé Knowles but she is still Kelly Rowland. And that's a lot to hope for. So I shifted my horizons again and decided that the person I actually wanted to be was Michelle Williams. The other one from Destiny's Child.

And for a while – aged ten – I was perfectly happy waking up each morning with the hope that, one day, I was magically going to turn into Michelle Williams.

But then I stopped being ten and became eleven. And with that extra year came wisdom. And I realized that it didn't actually make the slightest bit of difference whether I wanted to be Beyoncé or Kelly Rowland or Michelle Williams because I wasn't *ever* going to be any of them.

I'd always be Ronni Runnacles.

So I stopped dreaming impossible dreams and decided

that I'd like to be an astronaut instead. But then my dad told me that I'd need to work really hard in every single one of my science lessons and come first in every single science test forever. This was a shock because I hadn't realized that science and space were so connected. To be honest, I still don't see the link even now. But anyway, it put me off.

So I stopped wanting to be an astronaut and decided I'd quite like to be a lorry driver. And for at least a year, I dreamed of sitting high up above the traffic with my music playing really loud and RONNI written in great big letters right across the top of my windscreen. But then my mum told me that lorries are mostly driven by hairy men and that I'd be better off working in an office.

Since then, I haven't wanted to be anything. I suppose that's why I get so bored in my careers lessons.

And yesterday was the same. After I got out of English, I followed the crowd straight along the bottom corridor, around the corner and up the stairs, and along the top corridor to Lesson Three. I felt OK. I felt good about making it alive out of English. But within five minutes of sitting down in careers, I stopped feeling OK and good and started feeling thoroughly fed up again, because I could tell that this lesson was going to be just as awkward and as awful as everything else. And I knew it as soon as I looked at the leaflet that Dobby had shoved into my hand.

SO YOU WANT TO WORK IN... INSURANCE?

I looked at it for a second and then I handed it back to Dobby and said, 'Not really, thanks.'

Dobby isn't really called Dobby. She's **actually** called Mrs Flack and she's the careers and business studies teacher. Nobody ever calls her Mrs Flack though. Everybody calls her Dobby. Because she looks like a house-elf. She's quite small and thin and she wears big hand-knitted stripy jumpers and baggy leggings which flap around her ankles. And one time, she actually turned up to a lesson wearing two completely odd socks.

Dobby pulled a tissue out of the sleeve of her cardigan, rubbed her nose very vigorously, stuffed the tissue back up her sleeve and said, 'So what would you like to do?'

It was actually a really interesting question.

It

got

me

thinking . . .

'Well, that's actually a really interesting question and you've got me thinking,' I said, and smiled straight into the nearest television camera.

The American talk-show host flashed her dazzling white teeth at me and grinned. 'Thank you very much, honey, I aim to please.'

A ripple of laughter ran through the watching studio audience. The talk-show host – there had been so many that I'd forgotten her name – continued. 'But seriously, Ronni, you've now had three multi-platinum albums, you've dueted with Will.i.am, Shakira and Michael Bublé, and your latest album, *I'm Still Ronni From the Docks*, won a Nobel Peace Prize for its positive message to young people all over the world. So what *is* there left for you to achieve? What would you like to do next?'

'Oh, I just want to keep on doing my thing,' I said, and smiled shyly.

The studio audience erupted into massive applause.

'I just want to keep on doing my thing,' I said.

Somebody sniggered. I think it was probably Tamika Hardwick.

Dobby looked puzzled. And then she whipped her tissue out from her sleeve again, gave her nose a quick hard rub, put the tissue back in its hand-knitted home and said, 'I'm not sure that doing your thing is a viable career path, Veronica. There must be something that you picture yourself doing when you leave school?'

I stared at her and then I stared at the floor and then I shuffled around on my chair a bit and then I said, 'Not really.'

Dobby flicked a tiny flake of tissue paper from the end of her red nose and said, 'Don't close your mind to a possible future in insurance, Veronica. Insurance can be a very rewarding career. You could specialize in accountancy or risk management or loss adjusting or underwriting insurance claims . . . It really is an exciting and dynamic service industry.'

I couldn't tell whether she was being serious or not. I think she probably was.

Flooky was sitting next to me. Even though we haven't been getting on quite so well lately, we always sit next to each other.

She butted in and said, 'Be a property developer, Ronni. That's what I'm gonna be.'

'I dunno,' I said. 'I don't really fancy that either.' And it was true. Because what was the point of me wanting to be a property developer? Doing up scruffy houses might look like loads of fun on TV, but it still takes loads of money to buy a scruffy house in the first place. And my savings account only has £206 in it. It's not the same for Flooky. She'll get help. Her dad knows exactly how it's done. He owns loads of houses already.

Kelly Bugg was sitting opposite me. Even though I haven't been getting on very brilliantly with her either recently, we still always sit opposite each other. She'd been listening to mine and Flooky and Mrs Flack's conversation with a worried frown on her face. Now that the conversation was dipping a bit, she said, 'No offence, Ronni, but have you thought of being a Counter-intelligence Operative in the army? That's what I'm gonna do.'

I looked at her, surprised. From the corner of my eye, I think I could see Flooky and Mrs Flack doing the same thing. Kelly twirled a strand of her sandy hair anxiously round her little finger and said, 'I've been thinking about it a lot.'

'Oh,' I said.

I've known Kelly Bugg since we were both three years old and went to the same playgroup. But sometimes it really doesn't feel like that.

Kelly Bugg said, 'It's totally your decision, Ronni, but I could give you some details about it if you like?'

'Oh,' I said again. 'Thanks.' And then – because I wasn't exactly sure what a Counter-intelligence Operative actually did and because I was also pretty certain that I wouldn't be any good at it – I said, 'But . . . nah . . . I don't think so.'

Dobby looked at Flooky and Kelly Bugg and said, 'Well, it's excellent that you two both have such clear ideas. Well done, girls!' Then she looked at me and said, 'So now you need to follow the good example of your friends and identify what you want to do, Ronni. A clear focus will motivate you to succeed in your GCSEs. And good GCSEs will mean that there is a much better chance that you'll eventually find employment in your chosen field. It's what is known as a self-motivational success strategy.'

'Whoop,' I said.

Somebody sniggered again. I can't be sure but I'm 99.9 per cent certain that it was Tamika Hardwick.

Dobby said, 'There's no need to be like that, Veronica. We're very lucky living here. We have the docks on our doorstep. There are **all sorts** of exciting employment opportunities in a port. Have you ever thought about being an import-export clerk?'

I shifted around on my chair a bit more and then I said, 'Not really.' By now, I was practically **kicking myself** for not having just stayed in the bike shed with Stuart Bolan.

Dobby smiled. 'I tell you what we'll do, Ronni. We'll leave your friends to continue working on their Steps to Success Flow Charts and you can come and sit at my computer and complete an online psychological career test. That should help you identify the area of employment you're best suited for.' And she took out her flaky disintegrating tissue and attacked her nose again before adding, 'How does that sound to you?'

My stomach sank. But as Dobby was actually only trying to be nice I said 'Yeah, that sounds wicked and awesome. Thanks.'

Dobby looked pleased, fished a packet of Fisherman's Friends out from a big leather purse which was attached to her belt, popped a brown lozenge into her mouth and said, 'Wonderful. Come on then, let's get you started.'

So I left Flooky and Bugg to their flow charts and followed Dobby over to the computer. Once I'd sat down and logged on, she directed me to a website called www.workharder.com and said, 'Just complete the questionnaire, click SUBMIT and the website will do all the work for you and generate your ideal job. But, remember, Ronni, it's **very** important that your answers are honest. Give me a shout if you need any help.' And then she wandered off to speak to Stuart Bolan who had **finally** left the bike shed and appeared at the classroom door. He was looking cooler than Coolius Caesar but smelling like a volcanic ash cloud.

I sighed and looked at the screen.

The first question was not even a question. It was this:

Click on the <u>three</u> boxes that you think
describe you most accurately.

I immediately clicked *friendly*. Then I clicked *sensitive* because I am. And then I clicked *tactful* because of the way that I'd tactfully handled Dobby's career-test question.

The second question **was** a question. It was this:

> *Which working environment most appeals to you?*
>
> *Select one from the following list:*
>
> *Rural outdoors*   ●
>
> *Urban outdoors*   ●
>
> *A fixed confined space*   ●
>
> *A mobile confined space*   ●
>
> *A light and quiet room*   ●
>
> *A large room filled with voices*   ●
>
> *A dark room filled with music*   ●

I quickly scanned the list and then clicked on the final option. I didn't even need to think about it. Everybody loves parties.

The rest of the questions ran along the lines of this kind of thing:

Please click whether you strongly agree, agree, don't know, disagree or strongly disagree with the following statements:

	Strongly Agree	Agree	Don't Know	Disagree	Strongly Disagree
I am a very good listener.					
I am good at making other people feel calm.					
I cope well in stressful, upsetting situations.					

I moved quickly through the questions clicking *strongly agree* for everything and then I clicked SUBMIT. A wheel started spinning on the computer screen and a message told me to wait for my test results.

I pushed the mouse away and swung back on the two rear legs of my chair.

Dobby called over, 'Why aren't you doing that test, Veronica?'

'I've finished,' I said.

Dobby looked doubtful. 'Goodness! Already? That was quick. I'll be over in a second.' Then she turned her attention back to Stuart Bolan and I heard her say, 'Right, young man,

let's get you sorted out with one of my leaflets on import-
export clerks.'

The wheel on the computer screen stopped spinning and
the page reloaded. I clunked down on all four legs of my chair
and sat forward to see what my ideal job was. I was actually
quite excited. A dialogue box appeared in the middle of the
screen. It said this:

The www.workharder.com website has analysed
your responses to the workharder© psychological
career test and has concluded that your ideal job is:

an undertaker

Your answers suggest you are a good-natured person
who has the tact and sensitivity to communicate well
with people who have recently lost a close friend or
relative. You are reassuring, dependable and good in
situations that many others might find stressful. You
are comfortable in a dimly lit environment and prefer
the sound of soft classical music to the everyday
noise and bustle of the average workplace. You
are well-suited to working in a funeral
home.

Dobby appeared by my shoulder. She rubbed her nose frantically on her woolly sleeve and said, 'Does that help?'

'No' I said. 'It flipping well does not! I'm not working with dead people.'

Dobby dipped her fingers into her belt-bag for another Fisherman's Friend, popped one into her mouth and said, 'Look, Veronica, you don't need to make any final decisions on this right now. You're not even in Year 10 yet. But you do need to do some work this lesson – so can we just go with this undertaker idea for the time being and start thinking about producing an appropriate flow chart, please?'

'No,' I said. 'No way. I'm not being an undertaker. Not even for the purposes of a flipping flow chart.'

'Well then, you'd better think of something else fast,' snapped Dobby – just like a little angry elf. 'Because I do want to see some work from you by the end of the lesson.'

I sighed – and it was probably the deepest, noisiest and most thoroughly cheesed-off sigh that I'd breathed out that entire morning. In fact, if sighing was an Olympic sport, I'd have got a gold medal. And then I said the only thing that – in those circumstances – I could think of to say:

'Can you pass me that leaflet about insurance, please?'

Ronni Runnacles @ronneee_r

. . . and then something REALLY grabbed my goat.

Sadie Slowgrove looked at me wrong.

I was in the dining hall waiting to buy my baguette. At the front of the queue was Stuart Bolan and behind him was Tamika Hardwick and behind her was Sadie Slowgrove and behind her was Hannah-Michelle Peach and behind her was Kelly Bugg and behind her was Flooky – and behind Flooky was me. And I was just in the process of loading my tray up with a whopping great wedge of Victoria sandwich when I happened to look along the line and saw Sadie Slowgrove looking straight back at me. Our eyes met and, immediately, I was certain of one rock-solid fact.

She was looking at me wrong.

All wrong.

I know it doesn't sound a big deal. But it was. It was a bigger deal than lockless bathroom doors and bad homework and being told you'd make a good undertaker. It was even more of a big deal than the dock flame flickering and blowing out. Because, it was like she was looking at me and silently saying . . .

So I plonked the plate of Victoria sandwich down on my tray, glared back up the queue at her and said, 'Who the heck do you think you're staring at, Sadie Slowgrove?'

Everyone around us stopped bitching about the price of the tomato-ketchup sachets and went quiet. But only for a second. Because then Tamika Hardwick – who is incapable of keeping her mouth closed any longer than that – nudged Stuart Bolan and said, 'Watch this, Stu. Runnacles is about to go seriously off on one.'

Stuart Bolan stopped paying for his baguette, turned around and said, 'That girl is having such a random day. She told me her dad is a fancy scientist or something. Like that's even true! I'm sure my Uncle Gary once told me her dad drives a forklift on the docks.' And then he started laughing at me. Just for a change.

Tamika Hardwick said, 'Set your liar alarm. She'll be telling you Beyoncé is her cousin's best friend next.'

'Oh, shut your teeth,' I said. And then I caught sight of Sadie Slowgrove staring at me again and for some totally random reason that even I don't understand, I said, 'Did you just call me a liar?'

'No,' said Sadie Slowgrove.

And, even more randomly, I said, 'Yes you did. I flipping well saw you say it behind the back of your hand.'

'Liar,' said Sadie Slowgrove.

Dimly, in the background somewhere, I heard one of the dinner ladies say, 'Oi, cut it out, you kids. No argy bargy!'

Sadie Slowgrove's face had gone massively red. She picked up a bowl of jelly trifle from the chiller cabinet, held it in her hand like she was about to lob it at me and said, 'Anyway, was I actually looking at you in the first place? Was I actually even aware you were there?'

And I was a bit confused then. Because she definitely knew I was there all right. No doubt about it.

So I said, 'Too right you were! You were staring like a freaking zombie. Anyone would think I had a sign stuck to my head which says *Honk if you like what you see!*'

Dimly, in the background somewhere, I heard that same dinner lady say, 'Oi, oi, pack it in!'

Stuart Bolan called out, 'Go on, Runny Nose, sling the cake at her!' And then he looked at the dinner ladies and said, 'Joke.'

Flooky said, 'What the heck is going on?'

Sadie Slowgrove jiggled her bowl of trifle like it was a threat and said, 'If I'm a zombie, you're totally safe. Zombies only eat brains!'

And that was really annoying because I couldn't think of a good comeback. So instead, I just gritted my teeth and said, 'Oh, shut up, you silly sad cow!'

Sometimes it's probably best to say nothing.

And then a weird thing happened. Sadie Slowgrove suddenly seemed to grow older. She stood up straighter, looked me right in the eye and said, 'No, you're the sad one, Ronni. None of this is my fault. So stop making out that it is.'

And, loudly and hysterically, I said, 'No. It's not your fault, is it? It's your stupid tarty mum's fault!'

Sometimes it really is best to say nothing.

Stuart Bolan sneezed out a snort of laughter and said, 'You what?'

And Tamika Hardwick, Hannah-Michelle Peach, Kelly Bugg and Flooky all opened up their mouths and said . . .

'No offence, but . . .'

'What?'

'Huh?'

'Wot's this?'

and

'Come again?'

But not in any kind of organized way so that I could follow
their conversation. This sounded more like my brothers
shouting.

Dimly, in the background somewhere, I heard a very
annoyed dinner lady saying, 'Right. Out. The whole blinking
pack of you. If you can't queue for your lunch in peace, you can
all sling your flaming hooks.'

Sadie Slowgrove's face had gone all fuzzy and blurry. She

said, 'You leave my mum out of this.'

And I said, 'How the heck can I?' And then I made a weird hiccup noise because the lump that had been lurking in the back of my throat all morning had suddenly resurfaced and this time it was so big that I thought I was going to choke on it.

And it was at this precise moment that Sadie Slowgrove turned so completely fuzzy and blurry that I could hardly see her any more. In fact, I could hardly even see the plate of Victoria sandwich that I'd plonked on to my tray a minute or two earlier. So I took a couple of quick breaths, forced down the football in my throat and gratefully shoved my tray into the hands of the angry dinner lady who had miraculously appeared in front of me.

Then I turned around and stormed straight out of the dining hall. I had to. And it wasn't because I was worried about being thrown out. It was because I suddenly realized I was crying.

In front of the whole dinner queue.

Even in front of Stuart Bolan.

And as soon as this devastating fact fully dawned on me, I stopped sleepwalking around the school and headed for the seafront instead.

Ronni Runnacles @ronneee_r

There's something very fishy about
the sea. #fact

It doesn't add up.

It's just water. Miles and miles and miles of salty water. And it trembles and tumbles and seethes and shudders and heaves and shimmers and splashes and crashes. And it does that every second of every hour of every day and every night forever and ever.

Where does it get that kind of energy?

If anyone in my school had anywhere near that level of energy, the teachers would probably force them to do a whole heap of tests and then officially label them a crazy hyperpotamus. To be fair though, that person would probably get massively on my nerves.

But here's another weird thing. The sea never gets on my nerves.

There's something about it that calms me down and mellows me out. I can't explain how it works exactly, but it goes something like this: when I'm feeling cheesed off and wound up and hacked off and fed up, I sit by myself on the sea wall and just stare out at the horizon. And after a while I don't feel half as bad.

It's like the sea has somehow sucked all the bad vibes out of me and chucked them into the waves.

117

In the last month, I've sat on the sea wall a lot.

And yesterday, just after I ran out of the dining hall and legged it along the bottom corridor and darted into an empty classroom and snagged my tights clambering out through a window and sprinted across the schoolyard and ducked past Dobby who was doing a really bad job of guarding the school gates, that's where I found myself again.

On the sea wall. Just staring at the waves.

And luckily the rain had stopped and the sun was trying to force its way through the clouds. And even though it was still really rubbish weather considering that it's practically almost summer, the brown sea was sparkling and shimmering and shining and twinkling and looking ever so slightly like it might be some sort of greyish brown shade of blue.

So I sat there, swinging my legs and staring at it. And pretty soon all those bad vibes in my head and my belly gradually died down and disappeared.

But then the sun did too and the rain came back. So I hopped down from the wall and wandered over to the pier.

I love the pier almost as much as the sea. It's this big old wooden walkway on stilts and it starts on the promenade and takes you high over the beach and way out above the water.

And if you walk to the very end and look down between the gaps in the planks, you can actually see the waves way down beneath your feet and it makes you feel a bit sick and a bit worried. But I like that. Because all you have to do is look up again and something amazing happens. Instead of feeling sick and worried, you get this big buzz of excitement from the sudden realization that **you're actually only a boat ride away from anywhere**.

New York or Los Angeles could be just the other side of the horizon . . .

Like I said before, there's something fishy about the sea. Something I can't quite put my finger on. But there's something special about it too. And it's especially special when you're looking at it from the very end of the pier. But when I'm by myself, I don't tend to do that. I don't like the douchebags who sit there all day with their fishing rods and swear their heads off if you make the *slightest* sound.

I can't believe the fish give a monkey's. They don't even have ears.

So yesterday I stayed down the prom end. It's the end with the square white building on it and the double doors with these words painted on them:

WELCOME TO THE COPPER BOWL ON THE PIER

And for a while, I just stood there.

People were rushing in all directions into shops and cafes to escape the rain. Quite a few people were also rushing straight towards me. One of them was a big bald red-faced man who had written on his T-shirt. I think it was the name of a smelly metal band.

He stopped in front of me and said, 'Excuse me, sweetheart.'

'Oh,' I said, and stood aside so that he could get past. Then – as soon as he was through the door – I moved back again. Because it honestly wasn't raining quite so hard in that particular spot.

A seagull screeched, swooped down and perched on the railings. It put its head on one side and had a good look at me. Then it shook out its tail feathers, crapped out half its body weight in sloppy white bird poo and flew off again.

Two old women walked up. They were a lot like my nan but even less cool. One of them looked at me and said, 'Don't hover in the doorway, love. You're not a wasp. Are you going in or coming out?'

'Oh,' I said and stood there for a second – just hovering – while I thought about it.

The old woman rolled her eyes and said, 'Look, love – either buzz in or buzz off!'

She had a really bad attitude. I rolled my eyes back at her and said, 'All right, all right. I'm going in!'

'Well, thank goodness we got that established,' she snarked, and waved me forward. 'After you.'

So I pushed open the door and stepped in.

And even though I've been through the doors of the Copper Bowl on the Pier more times than I could possibly tell you, that's the only time I've ever been through them by myself. Because usually I'm with Flooky. Or Kelly Bugg. Or both of them. Or sometimes I'm with my mum and my brothers and my nan.

And up until a month ago I often went there with my dad too.

But yesterday it was just me. All on my own. And I was feeling a bit uncomfortable because I was a bit bothered about some of the douchebags who hang around in there all the time and look at you funny if you dare to play on their machine. But because it was now raining pretty hard, I put on my tough face and just went in anyway.

And, instantly, it was like

     stepping

              into

                       another

                              world.

The Copper Bowl on the Pier is a fuzzy world of semi-darkness and FLASHING SIGNS and MULTI-COLOURED LIGHTS

and **weird beeps** and the **chink chink chink** of *TUMBLING COINS* and a **mash-up** of INFECTIOUS LITTLE TUNES and a **million** other ALIEN SOUND EFFECTS.

And even though these noises might sound like the sort of tuneless racket that a smelly metal band called Hopeless Henchman would make, I could listen to them forever.

Because I love them.

Just like I love every inch of that entire place.

And so does every single *skipping*

skiving

shirking

bunking

bludging
wagging
ditching
mitching kid in my school.

Which means that truancy officers love the pier too.

But until yesterday I'd never actually seen one. And if you'd asked me to describe what a truancy officer looked like, I probably would have more or less described Mr Scrunton, the King of the Earwigs. But now I know they don't necessarily look anything like an earwig. They don't necessarily even look like a man.

I spotted her because she wasn't putting any coins into the machines. This isn't normal. In the Copper Bowl on the Pier, everyone is feeding the machines. And if they're not, it's because they've got no more coins to feed them with. So then everyone wanders around with their heads down and looks for random coins on the carpet. But this woman wasn't even doing that. She was just standing there. And whereas everyone else was dressed in jeans and hoodies and trainers and trackie bottoms, she was wearing proper trousers and proper shoes and a bright yellow anorak that said TRUANCY PATROL on the back. To be fair, I suppose she wasn't actually that tricky to spot.

She still nearly caught me though.

And the reason she nearly caught me is because my body was in the Copper Bowl but my brain was miles away.

Thousands   of

miles

away . . .

for railing lonely on the chart. But this wasn't just a event

that ... she was just chatting there. And where are you ...

. . . and I was wedged into the driving seat of a very nice shiny red sports car. My foot was pressing the accelerator hard to the floor and I was roaring through the California desert with the wind in my hair and hope in my heart. Loud music was pumping out of a pair of speakers placed right next to my ear and I was really loving it because it was actually a bootleg remix of my groundbreaking double-platinum multi-award-winning international Number One hit. So I shook back my sun-kissed hair and started singing,

'Roll up your sleeves, pull up your socks – Cos I'm still Ronni from the docks.'

And I must have been driving really fast – faster even than my nan does in her cheesemobile – because, within a matter of seconds, I'd left the California desert and was roaring through the streets of New York City. Big buildings were flashing by on either side of the road, and once or twice I got a glimpse of the Statue of Liberty sitting in the middle of an electric-blue bay.

And I'd never driven as well as this in my entire life. And even though the clock was ticking down dangerously I could see the finish line in the distance and I knew that I was actually going to reach it before those last few seconds disappeared.

But then a big yellow taxi pulled out of a side street and started weaving slowly down the road in front of me.

I panicked and looked at the clock. There were just four seconds left.

Drastic action was needed.

'Pull up your sleeves, roll up your socks – cos I'm still Ronni from the docks,' I said out loud to nobody.

And then I leaned forward, pressed the JUMP button on my dashboard and lifted off the ground and right up into the air and over that stupid slow-moving yellow taxi.

And I shouted, 'See you later, suckers!'

And then . . .

. . . I came crashing down again.

Bang on top of that stupid taxi.

My shiny red sports car burst into flames, the remaining seconds vanished from the clock and the GAME OVER sign flashed up on the screen.

'Flip,' I said. My hands felt sticky and dirty from the

steering wheel. I wiped them on my school blazer. And then, because I didn't have another 50p, I leaned forward and started to clamber out of the driving seat.

And that was when I saw her.

The woman who wasn't feeding the machines.

The woman with TRUANCY PATROL written in big giveaway letters on her back.

She was lurking next to a coin-drop machine called

2p OR NOT 2p

and even though she was facing the other way, I could tell from her lizard-like head movements that she was carefully checking out the entire arcade for escaped schoolkids.

In a panic, I crashed back down into my seat and hid my face in my hands. And then – realizing that this made me look as shifty as a sand dune – I forced my hands back on the steering wheel and pretended to play the game. For a few seconds I just sat there, sweating buckets inside my school uniform, and then I carefully turned my head and risked another glance into the danger zone.

She was still there, she was still swinging her head from side to side like a lizard and she still wasn't feeding the slots. She was also standing slap bang between me and the exit.

I bit my lip and stared at the message flashing on the screen in front of me.

PLEASE INSERT 50p TO PLAY

I wasn't actually reading it though. I was actually keeping very calm and trying to work out an escape plan.

Somebody's knuckles rapped on the roof of my car. I almost fell out of my skin.

A voice said, 'Don't hog the Burnout game, love. You're not Hamilton Button. Either put some money in the blinking thing or get out and let me and Sue have a spin.'

I looked up. Standing above me were the two old women I'd seen earlier. I breathed a sigh of relief. Putting on my tough face, I said, 'I'm not getting out. My 50p is stuck.'

The one who'd accused me of looking like a wasp said, 'The whole flipping world has got its money stuck. Don't you ever watch the news, love? The economy has gone belly up.'

And the other old woman – Sue – said, 'Come on, love, shift your Arsenal.'

'Goshhhh,' I muttered. 'What the heck is wrong with your generation?' But because I didn't want to cause a scene and because I knew I wouldn't win against these bad asses anyway, I surrendered and clambered out of the car. The Wasp Lady slipped straight into my place. She didn't even wait for the seat to cool down. As I hurried off, I heard her say to her friend, 'Don't look at me like that, Sue. It's my turn. You had a go earlier. Now shut your trap and let me have a crack at whipping this kid's high score.'

The truancy officer still had her back to me. I started walking straight towards her. It was a bold tactic, but it was the only tactic I had. I figured that if I walked quickly enough, I could be straight out through the doors before she even had a chance to twig that I was the only person in the whole place wearing a crap skirt and a bottle-green blazer.

I started walking.

The truancy officer looked down, stooped and picked a coin up from the floor.

I instantly stopped walking and chucked myself behind a machine called the Fortune Gumball Vendor.

The truancy officer turned round. She was now facing my direction. The only thing stopping her from seeing me was a mountain of fusty-looking gumballs. I crossed my fingers and crouched down a little. And, not for the first time in my life, I found myself sincerely wishing I was somebody else. Or just somewhere else. Because being caught skipping school isn't really a viable option when you've got a nan as hardcore as mine.

The truancy officer curled her hand round the coin and went back to moving her head very slowly from side to side looking for escaped schoolkids.

I stayed where I was, crouched low behind the fortune-telling gumballs. As long as I stayed where I was and she stayed where *she* was, I was safe.

A voice next to me said, 'Excuse me, sweetheart. Can I get to that gumball machine, please?'

I fell out of my skin. And then, looking up, I saw it was the big bald red-faced man with the weird T-shirt.

'I'm using it,' I said.

'No you're not,' said the Hopeless Henchman.

'Yes I am,' I said. And even though I was freaking out all over the place, I put on my toughest face ever and hoped he'd just get the message and go away.

'Steady on, love,' he said, 'There's no need to look at me like that. It's not your machine. You don't own it.'

'Oh yeah,' I said, 'and how do you know that exactly?' It was a pretty stupid challenge, but I was getting desperate.

The Hopeless Henchman raised his eyebrows and said, 'Let's just say there's more to me than meets the eye.'

I stared at him. And then I muttered, 'Goshhhh. Keep your fusty flipping gumballs!' And knowing I really couldn't hide there any longer, I took a deep breath and just accepted the fact that my day was about to get a whole lot worse and that my nan was probably going to kill me when she found out I'd been skipping school.

I stepped out from the shelter of the gumballs and looked up. The truancy officer was still facing my way and standing between me and the exit. But instead of searching for escaped schoolkids, she was feeding a coin into one of the slot machines.

I had about three seconds to save my life.

I looked at the double doors. Part of me wanted to run for it and part of me was suddenly way too scared. The scared part of me was winning. Desperately, I looked left. I saw the old ladies in the racing car. Even more desperately, I looked right. I saw those fusty fortune-telling gumballs again. And then –

just when all hope seemed to be lost – something sparked inside my head. And I suddenly remembered someone who could help me. In fact, I've got no idea how I ever managed to forget her in the first place. Because she absolutely isn't the forgettable type. She's one of those people who floats around in your head forever like space junk.

Very carefully and very slowly, I backed away. And I kept on carefully and slowly backing away until I was in the furthest corner of the arcade. And when I got to that corner I found myself standing next to a little purple kiosk with this sign on it:

SEASIDE SIBYL WORLD-FAMOUS FORTUNE-TELLER

Seaside Sibyl is not just a World-Famous Fortune-Teller, Seaside Sibyl is also my oldest friend. I know we're friends because she always says hello to me and, also, she's one of my seven followers on Twitter. But yesterday I temporarily forgot she existed. I suppose I just had too much other stuff on my mind.

I put my mouth close to the silvery curtain of her kiosk and called, 'Hello. Is it OK to come in?'

A familiar gravelly voice called back, 'Yeah, come on in. There's nobody with me. Living or dead.'

I pushed back the curtain and ducked inside.

Seaside Sibyl is a local legend. She's got a crystal ball and tarot cards and makes her clients cups of tea with proper tea leaves in, and then – when they've drunk it all down – she reads them the future from right out of the bottom of their cup. Her kind of fortune-telling is worlds apart from the fake banter you get wrapped around a fusty bit of gum from a gumball machine.

When I went in, she was doing her make-up. She'd taken off the sparkly silver headscarf that she almost always wears and was drawing on a pair of jet-black eyebrows with an eyebrow pencil. As soon as she saw me, she lowered her pencil, smiled a massive gold-toothed smile and said, 'Hello, Ronni, my little peanut. Long time no see.' And then she stopped smiling, did a weird one-eyebrowed frown and added, 'Shouldn't you be at school?'

I've known Seaside Sibyl all my life. But she hasn't known me all of hers because she was at least fifty by the time I was born. And that's how come she's my oldest friend.

She's also the only one of my friends who would team a

silky leopard-print blouse with a purple velvet cloak.

I sat down in the empty chair opposite her. 'It's a teacher-training day,' I said. 'I didn't have to go in.' There was a narrow gap where the curtain didn't quite reach the edge of the doorway. Through that narrow gap I could see the truancy officer. She was still lurking about near that dumb gumball machine.

Sibyl picked her pencil back up and finished the job she'd started. 'You're putting me in an awkward position, kiddo,' she said. And she frowned again. But this time it didn't look quite so weird because she had the normal number of eyebrows.

'Honestly,' I said, 'it is. The teachers are learning how to engage us.'

Sibyl stared at me. She has the bluest eyes of anyone I've ever met. I don't even think they're contact lenses. She kept on staring at me and said, 'So that's why you're wearing school uniform, is it?'

'Oh,' I said.

She shook her head, picked up a hand mirror and checked out her drawing skills. Then she passed the mirror to me and said, 'Hold that still while I pop my lippy on.'

I did as I was told. Sibyl picked a tube out of her make-up

bag and smeared her lips in a thick glossy layer of dark red lipstick.

'You can put that down now.'

I put the mirror down.

Dabbing at her lips with a hanky, Seaside Sibyl said, 'And what do I say to your nana next time I see her? Hey? Do I say you've been in the arcade – skipping school – or do I keep *shtum* and pretend I haven't clapped eyes on you?'

My nan has also known Seaside Sibyl forever. They've been next-door neighbours since the fossils were alive. And if my nan hadn't rocked up at our house and taken possession of the sofa bed, they'd still be neighbours now.

'Can you keep *shtum*, please?' I said. 'You know what she's like. She'd only go ballistic and crash her cheesemobile or something.'

Sibyl raised her newly drawn eyebrows and then she raised a finger too and started wagging it at me. 'Now looky here,' she said. 'Your nan is all right. I've known her donkey's years. And she's always telling me you're her favourite granddaughter. She wouldn't give you grief unless you were making a nuisance of yourself.'

'Goshhhh,' I said. And then I just looked at the floor

and wished I was someone else.

Or *somewhere* else.

But I didn't get up and leave. I couldn't, could I? Not while the child-catcher was still on the prowl. I sneaked a glance through the gap in the curtain again. Yep. There she was.

Sibyl stopped wagging her finger at me, pulled her purple cloak tighter around her shoulders and said, 'As much as I'm tickled pink to see you, Ronni, I can't have you in here during school hours. You'll get me booted off the pier. So let's just say our goodbyes and maybe you'll come back some other time.'

'Goshhhh,' I said again. And then, properly panicked, I lowered my voice and said, 'You can't kick me out. Not yet.'

The truancy officer was only a metre or so away. I felt sick.

Sibyl's eyes narrowed and she pressed her new red lips hard together. Something told me that the next thing she said was going to be very important to me – one way or another. Maybe I'm a fortune-teller too.

I crossed my fingers and held my breath.

All the tension in Seaside Sibyl's face suddenly drained away. I sat forward in my seat, still not breathing. She looked relaxed and dreamy. In a matching dreamy voice, she said, 'I have a hunch that something is causing you great stress.'

I uncrossed my fingers and breathed out noisily. And then I thought about all the crap that's been going on in my life recently and mumbled, 'A bit, yeah.'

Seaside Sibyl immediately stopped looking dreamy, sat back in her seat and looked pleased. 'I knew it,' she said in her normal growl. 'My hunches are never wrong. I've got a gift, you see.'

I didn't say anything. I was finding it all a bit weird.

She stood up, reached around to a teapot on the shelf behind her and said, 'I tell you what I'll do. I'll make us a nice cup of tea and you can tell me all about it. I shouldn't really. I'll be booted out if anyone realizes I'm harbouring an escaped schoolkid in here.'

And for one horrible second, I thought she was going to change her mind and just chuck me out anyway. The weirdness stopped being an issue.

But then she shrugged and said, 'If a customer comes along and wants a reading or needs me to chat to a dead relative, you'll have to hop it. I'm a fortune-teller, not a flaming youth club. You got that?'

'Totally,' I said, and tried not to think about her chatting to dead people.

Sibyl clattered some cups around. I sat and waited anxiously and crossed my fingers again and hoped that the child-hunter outside wouldn't come barging in with a search warrant. Through that handy gap in the curtains, I could see that the distance between us had grown a bit. Ever so slightly, I relaxed.

Seaside Sibyl plonked a teapot and two cups down on the table. 'Pour your own,' she said, and nodded at the teapot. 'It's bad luck if I do it. It'd be no different to pouring water over all your hopes and dreams.'

'Oh,' I said. 'Right.' And I quickly did as I was told. Something about Seaside Sibyl makes you do that. Then I said, 'Have you got any milk?'

Sibyl didn't answer me straight away. Instead, she pulled her purple shawl tighter round her shoulders, dipped a hand inside her silky leopard-print blouse and pulled out the silver headscarf which is almost always on her head. And then she put it on. The transformation was instant and magical. She looked like a chocolate bar. Looking at me with her bright blue eyes, she said, 'Milk is for milkshakes.'

I sat forward, startled. The dreamy voice was back again.

Sibyl continued, 'But tea is for telling the future.'

'Oh,' I said. 'Right.'

Seaside Sibyl lifted her own cup, moved it through the air in slow careful circles so that the tea sploshed around inside and then raised it to her lips and downed the whole lot in one big noisy slurp.

'Crikey,' I said. 'You were thirsty.'

'And now you,' she said, still with that freaky dreamy voice.

I picked up my cup, jiggled it about a bit and took a sip.

'**Urgghh,**' I said. And then, remembering my manners, I said, 'It's cold.'

'I want the tea leaves to talk,' said Sibyl. 'Not scream.'

'Oh,' I said. 'Right.' And trying not to worry too much about the rank way it tasted, I drank it straight down just as Sibyl had done.

Seaside Sibyl waggled her finger at me and I gave her my cup. She placed it on the table in front of her, placed her elbows on the table too and rested her forehead on her fingertips. And then she stared down into the cup and started muttering to herself and rocking backwards and forwards. And pretty soon she wasn't muttering at all, she was actually talking very loudly and saying things like this:

'Well I never.'

'**Ooooooh.**'

'Aha!'

'Crikey!'

'Ha!'

And then she stopped rocking, sat back in her chair and said,

'Flaming typical!'

I leaned forward across the table. I was so **engaged** I think I'd forgotten to breathe. I never feel like this in school. Mrs Booley and Dobby the house-elf could learn a lot from Seaside Sibyl. 'What is it?' I said. 'What did the tea leaves say?'

'Be careful what you wish for,' said Sibyl.

'Oh,' I said. 'Right. What else?'

'That's it,' said Sibyl. 'Be careful what you wish for.'

I looked at her. 'That's it?'

'Yep,' she said. 'That's your lot. Damn good advice as well.'

'That's **seriously** it?' I said. 'But you were looking into that cup for ages.'

Sibyl shrugged. 'It ain't easy, Ronni. Even with my gift.'

'Goshhhh,' I said. 'I feel like I've been robbed!'

Sibyl sat back in her chair and looked surprised. Then she wagged her finger at me. 'Now looky here,' she said. '*I* don't decide what's in the tea leaves. Only destiny decides. And just you remember something, Ronni – you haven't been robbed because you haven't paid.' Then she stopped wagging her finger, poured herself another cup of tea and said, 'Now why don't you tell me what's been troubling you?'

But looking through that little gap in the curtains, I spotted something which instantly made my whole world seem brighter. The truancy officer was disappearing through the doors. Feeling massively more cheerful, I smiled and stood up. 'It's all right,' I said. 'I'm OK now. But thanks for the tea.'

Seaside Sibyl didn't smile back. She just looked at me with her big blue intense eyes and said – kind of frostily – 'And what about the message I read in the leaves? Aren't you going to thank me for that too?'

'Oh,' I said. 'Yeah. Cheers, Sibyl.' And knowing that the coast was clear, I smiled again and said, 'See you later.'

But still Seaside Sibyl did not smile back.

Ronni Runnacles @ronneee_r
A smile is something you can't give away. It *always* comes back to you.

Or so my nan says.

Until yesterday, I just thought this was a load of

extra-mature

vacuum-packed

foil-wrapped

full-fat

easy-squeeze

spreadable

cheese.

And it's very hard to know how to react to something you think is as cheesy as that. So whenever she's said it I've mostly stuck to the same response. I've pulled a face, picked up my phone and said something like, 'I'm going to tweet that, Nan.' And that's usually made her pipe down.

But yesterday, as I hurried up the promenade and away from the Copper Bowl on the Pier, I found myself mulling over her cheesy words of wisdom. And pretty soon a very intense question started to take shape in my mind. It was this:

> If I'd just given Seaside Sibyl a full set of my smiles, *why* had she frozen me out with a face like a fusty gumball?

A smile should always come back to you. My nan reckons that. And she might be a hardcore control freak, but she's also got this annoying habit of being right about practically everything. Take last Christmas for example. She came over on Boxing Day and while we were having our tea she said, 'You should lay off those pickled onions, Ronni, or you'll regret it.'

And I said, 'No I won't.' And I carried on eating them and pretty much polished off the whole jar.

But it turned out that my nan was right. I *did* regret it. And so did everyone else who was trapped in the house with me.

So – to get back to the smiling thing – what I'm saying is this: Either

     a) my nan was wrong for once

     or

     b) I hadn't actually been smiling. I'd just been bending my mouth a bit.

I sort of think it was (b).

And this worried me because I suspected that I'd been doing a fair bit of that in the past month. Just bending my mouth without really feeling anything. And sometimes I'd even added ha ha ha sound effects simply for the hell of it. But I still hadn't really been feeling anything. Other than a bit fed up. And a lot left behind. And totally on my own. In actual fact, my smiles were no more real than the painted-on smile of a clown. And thinking about this sort of wrecked my mood.

So I switched channels and started thinking about something else instead.

'And tonight's final guest is Ronni Runaway!'

The studio audience cheered. Another audience. Another talk show. I walked on to the set, smiled and blew everyone a kiss. And then I shook hands with the host, said hi to the other celebritites on the sofa and sat down.

Next to me, Robert Pattinson said, 'Wow.This is like a dream come true. I can't believe I'm sitting on a sofa with Ronni Runaway!'

I laughed, flicked back my hair and batted my lashes at him. 'Rob, you are SOOO sweet,' I purred.

At the other end of the sofa, Katy Perry looked well jealous.

The host of the show said, 'So, Ronni, how is life for you at the moment?'

'Amazing,' I said. 'I'm blessed. My life is amazing.'

My host gave me a syrupy smile. 'Wonderful. That's absolutely wonderful. And I'm sure we'd all agree with that. Did you know that you're now the most followed person on the whole of Twitter?'

'No, I didn't know that,' I said. And I glanced along the sofa and smiled at Katy Perry, who was looking fed up.

'You're really an inspiration,' said the talk-show host. And he smiled into the nearest camera and started telling all the people watching at home exactly how brilliant I was.

But I wasn't listening. I was too busy trying to remember what this guy's name was. One of the production crew had told me but I'd forgotten. It wasn't my fault – this was my fifth television appearance of the day . . .

A grumpy voice in front of me said, 'You're the fifth kid I've seen skipping school today. You lot are throwing away your education.'

Startled, I looked up. The speaker had slicked-back rockabilly hair, shaggy L-shaped sideburns and a little round earring in one ear. He was sheltering under a massive brolly and standing next to a rain-drenched bouncy castle. I know that castle. My nan took me and Ryan to jump around on it the day that Brother Number Two – Jack – was born. I hadn't liked it though because the castle smelt really badly of warm plastic and sweaty feet.

The grumpy man under the brolly was Bouncy Castle Ken.

The Man Who Honked.

I stared at him in surprise and then I said, 'What's it got to do with you?'

'A fair amount,' said Bouncy Castle Ken. 'Because you're sitting on my wall.'

I looked down at the little brick wall I was sitting on. It separated the bouncy-castle play area from the pebble beach. I'd been so busy thinking about my secret celebrity life that I wasn't even aware I'd stopped walking and parked my bottom on it.

In deliberate slow motion, I pulled the scrunchy out of my wet hair and re-threaded my ponytail. And then I shrugged, put on my tough face and said, 'It's a wall. I can sit here if I like.' And then I shivered because I had raindrops dripping down the back of my neck.

Bouncy Castle Ken said, 'I pay rent for that wall. And I want parents of young kiddies to sit on it while they watch their nippers having fun. I don't want teenage nuisances like you sitting there. You'll put me out of business. So hop it.'

I didn't know what to say so I toughed it out and kept on staring at him. But to my horror he started to go a bit fuzzy and blurry at the edges. In a panic, I quickly looked, wiped my eyes with the back of my hand and said, 'Goshhhh. No wonder my nan won't let you squeeze her flipping toothpaste!' And then I sprang down from his stupid precious wall and scarpered. And I didn't stop scarpering until I reached the gates of Reggie Branning's Amusement Park.

Reggie Branning's Amusement Park is another place I like. It's right at the end of the prom and it fills a big square of land jammed between the sand dunes and the ancient fort. Behind the blue entrance gates there's a wooden roller coaster

151

called the Mad Mouse. The Mad Mouse doesn't have any loop-the-loops or corkscrew twists or sudden death drops but it's still the scariest roller coaster I've ever been on. When you're moving really fast, the entire frame shakes and rattles. And written in big letters on the handrail of every car is a sign that says:

SCREAM IF YOU WANT TO GO FASTER

Further into the park, there are lethal-looking chair-o-planes. And an ancient helter-skelter. And a really lame ghost train. And a crazy house that is completely empty except for a few murky mirrors that deliberately make you look fat. And a big-dipper slide that is actually not all that big. And coconut shies. And rifle ranges. And hoopla stalls. And fading red waltzers that spin round really fast to the sound of blisteringly loud heavy metal music.

To be honest, I can take or leave all these things.

But at the back of the park – where the rides are under cover and where the heavy metal music is played even louder – is my favourite attraction of all.

The dodgem track.

I've always loved the dodgems. Me and Flooky and Kelly Bugg have been driving those cars and bumping them together since we were *this* tall:

ALL DRIVERS MUST BE THIS TALL.

And before that we'd sit next to our accompanying adults and try to keep still while *they* did the driving. Usually, my accompanying adult would be my nan – who drove surprisingly slowly considering how fast she drives her cheesemobile. But other times I'd sit next to my dad and he'd hold on to me tightly and deliberately drive us in the wrong direction so that we could have the biggest bumps of all. And the bigger the bump the more I loved it. Even though head-on bumping is strictly against the rules.

And now, all by myself, I leaned against the barrier of the track and watched a few very sensibly driven dodgems going round and round under flashing orange strobe lights. And for a second, I thought about my dad and how totally brilliant it was when we used to go round and round that track the wrong way.

The bumper cars in front of me fuzzed up and turned blurry.

I looked down at the ground and muttered, 'Goshhhh.' And then I put on my tough face, did some intense speed-blinking and looked up again. And to my complete and utter astonishment, I saw Stuart Bolan driving straight towards me.

I don't know how I ever missed him. He wasn't driving sensibly like everyone else – he was zigzagging about like a demented Dalek. And his bottle-bleached fringe had blown upwards, highlighting the fact that he was easily the best-looking person on the dodgem track. And, to be honest, he stood out anyway. Because – apart from me – he was the only person in the whole of Reggie Branning's Amusement Park wearing a bottle-green blazer. Evidently, he was even worse at staying in school than I was.

Stuart Bolan took one hand off his steering wheel and waved at me.

I crossed my arms over the barrier and lowered my chin on to them. The last time I'd seen Stuart, he'd been standing in the dinner queue and laughing his head off at my expense.

Stuart took his other hand off the steering wheel and gave me a big double-strength wave.

I shrugged a hello but didn't bother to lift my head up.

Stuart shouted something. I couldn't hear what it was because of the blisteringly loud heavy metal.

I shrugged an I-can't-hear-you.

Stuart Bolan stood up in his dodgem, cupped his hands around his mouth and yelled, 'Get in a dodgem!'

Almost immediately, the music stopped pumping, the orange lights stopped flickering and a very loud foreign-sounding voice said,

'Yes. Sit down!'

Stuart flicked a V-sign at the dodgem man's kiosk, thumped back down into his seat and zig-zagged onwards.

The heavy metal started up again and the orange lights began to flash.

I watched as Stuart bashed really hard into the side of a car being driven by an old woman who looked a bit like my nan. There are a lot of women with that look in this town.

The old woman turned round and shouted something very shocking at Stuart. He laughed and blew her a kiss. And even though he'd more or less called me a liar earlier, *I* laughed too. I know it sounds shallow, but Stuart Bolan really is exceptionally good-looking. I think his face took the edge off my grudge.

And all of a sudden I didn't just want to stand there watching things happen. Hadn't I done enough of that already? Hadn't I spent my entire life watching my parents scream and shout at each other and then smile and act as if nothing had happened? And hadn't I grown up watching my brothers fart and burp and crack their knuckles and click their jaws and bum-bump down the stairs and play the armpit accordion and pretend to be Lionel Messi or Lord Voldemort or Usain Bolt or a ninja? And hadn't I watched my mum sit in the kitchen and cry every day for the past month?

I felt like I was due a bit of action.

Stuart Bolan cupped his hands together again and shouted, 'Come on!'

I stood up and slapped my pockets. I don't know why. I knew full well there was nothing in them. I'd used my last 50p playing Burnout.

Stuart waved at me to join him. I pointlessly patted my pockets again. And then I looked down at the ground to see if I could spot a random 50p. I couldn't. So I looked up again and glanced about desperately and

to
my
complete
and
utter
astonishment,

I saw Yuri Maximovich Krolik.

The Spaceman.

He was standing by the kiosk and talking to a spotty guy in a brown-and-orange staff uniform. I could tell it was Yuri because he had the handles of his sports bag wrapped around his forehead.

I waved at him.

Yuri Maximovich Krolik and the spotty guy stopped talking to each other and stared at me.

'Goshhhh,' I muttered. 'What the heck is wrong with everyone?' And then, because I really didn't have any better ideas, I hurried over.

'Hi,' I said to Yuri. I looked at the spotty guy and gave him a quick nod. I'm not good with random strangers.

Yuri frowned, mumbled something in Russian, took his bag off his head, smoothed down his hair and eventually said, 'Yes hello.'

'Yes hello,' I said straight back. Completely pointlessly.

Yuri said, 'Yes, I introduce you to my brother, Misha.' And he looked at the spotty guy and said, 'Yes, I introduce you to girl from school. Ronni Runnacle.'

'RunnacleS,' I said quickly. And I laughed really lamely and said, 'I've got more than one Runnacle.'

Yuri and his brother both frowned.

'Forget it,' I mumbled.

Misha nodded at me, sniffed loudly and said, 'Yes hello.' And then he mumbled something in Russian too, sniffed again and went back inside the kiosk.

Yuri looked at me. 'Yes. Should you have supposed to being in school?'

'That's rich,' I said. 'Shouldn't you be as well?'

Yuri shrugged. 'Yes but Mr Scrunton is giving me special permissions to collect forgotten dinner money from brother Misha.'

'Oh,' I said. And then I paused a moment before adding, 'Will your brother let me on the dodgems for free?'

'No,' said Yuri.

'Oh,' I said. And then I paused again. 'Will he let you on for free?'

'Yes,' said Yuri.

'Whoop,' I said. 'He wouldn't be able to do that if he had a boring old job in insurance, would he?'

Yuri looked confused and then wobbled his head as if he couldn't decide whether to nod or shake it.

Pushing my hand into the pocket of my blazer, I crossed my fingers and said, 'Do you fancy having a go? And I'll sit next to you if that's OK. That way I won't have to pay.'

Yuri thought about it. Then he said, 'No.'

I turned and looked back over the barrier. Stuart Bolan was still driving like a demented Dalek and still being good-looking.

'Oh, go on,' I said. 'It'll be a laugh.'

159

Yuri thought about it. And then he shook his head and said, 'No. I am not thinking so.'

I sighed. 'Just *one* go. I'll even drive if you like.'

Yuri's eyes flickered over to the dodgems. It was just a hunch, but I got the impression he was weakening. After another second or so, he said, 'Yes but I'm not sure. I am wanting to go back to school and learn about fat king with many wives in history lesson. I am not wanting to be late.'

I looked at my watch. 'You're late now anyway. The lunch period finished five years ago.'

Yuri looked alarmed. 'I made solemn promise to Mr Scrunton.'

'Don't worry about him,' I said. 'He thinks he's it, but actually he's just an earwig.'

Yuri looked massively confused. And then he said, 'Yes.' And then – for the first time ever – he smiled.

And because it shouldn't be possible to give away a smile, I smiled back at him.

'Come on,' I said. 'Just one go. Please.'

Yuri scratched his head. Something told me that the next thing he said was going to be very important – one way or another. Finally, he said, 'OK, I am making you serious offer. I go on dodgems with you if you make solemn promise to come back to school with me straight afterwards.'

'Oh God,' I said. 'That's the worst offer I've ever heard!'

'Yes but OK,' said Yuri. 'You take or you leave.' And he picked up his bag, put the straps over his head and started to walk off.

A movement in the corner of my eye made me turn my head. Stuart Bolan was waving at me again.

'Wait,' I called. 'Hang on, Yuri.'

Yuri stopped.

'OK. That's cool. I promise. One go and then we'll go back to school.'

'Yes,' said Yuri. And he walked back to the kiosk and said something in Russian to Misha. Seconds later, we were both on the other side of the barrier.

That doesn't happen if your brother is an insurance clerk.

The heavy metal music faded, the orange lights disappeared and the dodgems all slowed to a stop. Magnified a million times by the speakers, I heard the sound of a human sniff. Then Misha's voice said,

'Yes. Get out, please. Unless you pay for double ride.'

A couple of people clambered out of their cars. Stuart Bolan stayed where he was and waved his double-ride ticket in the air.

Yuri started to walk towards an orange car with a number seven painted on the front. I grabbed him by the arm and said, 'No, let's get that one. It's really fast.' And I pointed to an electric-blue bumper car with a number three painted on it. I always choose the blue number three if I can. It's the one my dad used to drive the wrong way round the track. He nodded and we both ran over to it. I was about to hop inside, but then I hesitated and said, 'Do you want to drive?' And then I crossed my fingers behind my back.

'Yes but no,' said Yuri. 'You do it.'

'Whoop,' I said, and clambered in behind the steering wheel. Yuri climbed in next to me.

I pushed down the foot pedal and waited.

The rock music returned. So did the orange lights. The low ceiling above our heads lit up with white sparks and the air filled with the smell of burning electricity. My fast blue car crept forward and then began to pick up some serious pace.

Stuart Bolan was a few metres ahead of us. I kept my foot flat to the floor and steered after him. The gap between us was closing. I knew Blue Number Three was faster than the rest. I knew I could catch him.

Suddenly there was a massive **thump**, our car jumped sideways, my foot bounced off the pedal and we came to a stop.

Yuri said, '**Argh**,' and grabbed on to the handlebar in front of his seat.

I looked round to see who had bumped us. It was that old lady. One of the legions of genetically modified nans. Clearly she was less sensible than I'd suspected.

'Gotcha,' she shouted.

I laughed.

Yuri shook his head and spoke into my ear. 'I am not liking this.'

'No way,' I said. 'How can you not like the dodgems? You are so random, Yuri.'

Yuri didn't say anything.

I put my foot back on the pedal and we moved forward again. I looked around. I'd lost sight of Stuart Bolan.

Bump.

We lurched forward. Yuri's fists clenched tighter on the handlebar. I looked behind. Stuart Bolan was sitting in his dodgem and laughing. I laughed too and waved.

Yuri looked to see who I was waving at and then shook his head and said, 'I am not liking him.'

'No way,' I said. 'How can you not like Stuart Bolan? He's sooo cool!'

Yuri didn't say anything.

Stuart Bolan pulled up level with us. He was still laughing. His bottle-bleached fringe had blown up into a quiff and the badges on his blazer were sparkling with the reflected light from the flashes of electricity on the ceiling. He was way the best-looking person on the dodgem track. Leaning dangerously out of his car, he shouted, 'This *soooo* beats double science!'

And I guess I must have forgotten which channel I was tuned into because I opened up my mouth and shouted, 'Nice bumping, Stu. Don't I get blown a kiss now?'

I actually said it out loud. It wasn't in my head or anything.

Stuart Bolan ran one hand through his quiff, pulled a face and said, 'Dream on, Runny Nose. I'd rather kiss your nan.' And then he said, 'Joke,' and drove off.

And for a second I just sat there – in a dodgem with the Spaceman – and felt thoroughly confused. But then I stopped feeling confused and just thought

Oh my God!
I'm a
total loser!

And after that I closed my eyes and wished I was someone else. Or at least somewhere else.

Yuri said, 'Yes, I am thinking this boy is total loser.' It was like he'd read my mind. Almost.

Surprised, I opened my eyes again and turned my head sideways. Yuri shrugged and gave me a small awkward smile. It was a nice smile though. So I smiled back.

'Come on, Yuri, let's get him,' I said. And I pushed my foot down on the pedal.

Yuri said, 'Yes but I am not liking this idea.'

I didn't say anything. I was too focused on the chase.

But the gap between me and Stuart was too much. Even in

the super-fast Blue Number Three, I knew I'd never catch him.

So I did something drastic.

I turned the wheel of my car hard to the right and spun the dodgem round until we'd done a 180-degree spin. And then I put my foot down hard and started driving up the track in the wrong direction.

Next to me, I felt Yuri stiffen. He nudged my arm and pointed to a sign attached to the barrier.

ONE DIRECTION ONLY. NO HEAD-ON BUMPING!

'YEAH YEAH BIG WHOOP,' I said. And I just carried on going the wrong way, and every second the Speedy Little Blue Number Three was getting faster and faster and faster. Dimly, in the background somewhere, I was aware of a voice over the loudspeaker telling me to stop.

But I didn't stop.

I turned a corner of the track and there he was. Stuart Bolan. The coolest person in my school. Probably the coolest person in my town. Maybe even the coolest person in the world. But not the coolest person on that dodgem track. No way.

Our eyes met. For a second, he looked shocked. But then he grinned, leaned forward into his steering wheel for maximum aerodynamics and kept on coming **straight towards me.**

Yuri tugged my arm. 'Stop!'

In the background somewhere, I heard a voice over the loud speaker saying the same thing.

But I didn't stop.

Instead, I leaned forward into the steering wheel too and lifted my bum up from my seat so that I could put every ounce of weight on to the power pedal. I was going to show Stuart Bolan **exactly** who he was dealing with.

Miss Ronni Runaway.

Pop sensation.

Teen idol.

Queen of the TV chat show.

Star of the Pyramid stage.

Friend of will.i.am, Shakira, Michael Bublé, Beyoncé, Jay-Z and that man from Coldplay.

And Supreme Ruler of Reggie Branning's dodg e m tr a ck

167

And **that's** when it happened.

That weird thing I mentioned way back at the beginning.

And I don't remember a bump.

And I don't remember the heavy metal music stopping.

I don't even remember somersaulting straight over the steering wheel of the speedy little Blue Number Three.

I just remember staring at the flickering orange lights of the dodgem track. And then I sat up and rubbed my head and felt really **seriously** weird. And Stuart Bolan was sitting next to me and rubbing his head as well. When he saw me staring at him, he glared back and said, '**What the heck did you do that for?**'

And suddenly I started feeling even weirder still.

Because it began to dawn on me that something wasn't right. In fact, it began to dawn on me that everything had turned

TOTALLY UPSIDE DOWN.

And because this really isn't any ordinary sort of story and because things don't always unfold exactly how you expect, I now need you to turn this book upside down, flick back until you find page 170 and pick up the action from there.

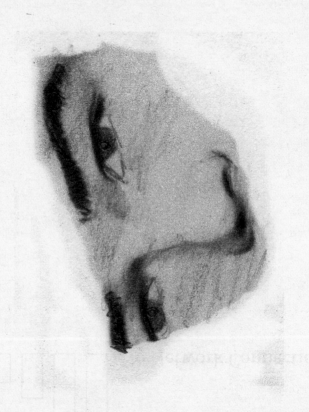

No Network Connection.

'Ronni, can you look this way, please?'

Still rubbing my head, I turned to see who was calling me, but shrank back as a billion blinding white lights flashed in front of my eyes. For a few seconds, all I could see was this:

Then, somebody grabbed hold of my arm.

'Back off, douchebag,' I snapped. And I shook myself free and curled into a tight prickly ball like a hedgehog. I know this isn't exactly normal behaviour, but try not to judge me too harshly. The entire concept of normal had suddenly vacated the planet.

The strange hand backed off and a voice muttered, 'Flipping diva!'

Someone else shouted, 'Ronni . . . Ronni . . . Can you look at me, please?'

My head was full of fog. I shook it. The fog swirled faster and thicker like one of those miniature snow

scenes you get trapped inside a glass ball.

'Ronni . . . Ronni . . .'

There were so many voices everywhere. They were
all over the place
and it was making me really dizzy.

'Ronni . . .'

Another hand touched my arm. Or maybe it was the
same hand as before. Either way, I flinched again and
waited for the fog to lift. After just a few more seconds,
the white blizzard stopped swirling and my mind grew
clearer and clearer until, pretty soon, all that was left was
one single thought:

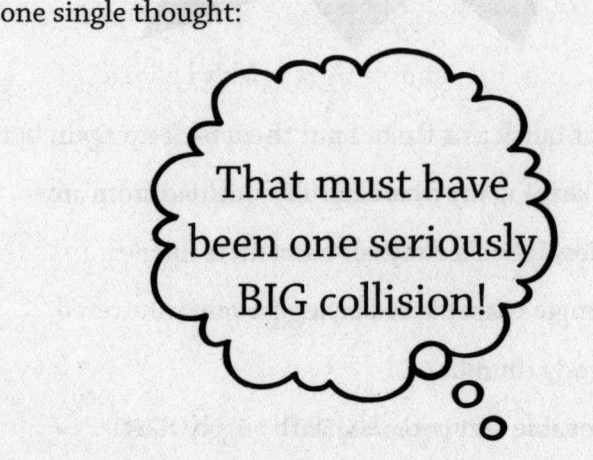

That must have
been one seriously
BIG collision!

I held my breath and ran my fingers over my face to check
out my latest facial situation.

Two non-bleeding eyebrows ✔

One non-bleeding nose ✔

Two non-bleeding ears ✔

I breathed out an enormous sigh of relief and lowered my
hands.

Not quite as quick as a flash, I put them back up again.
And then, keeping my eyes carefully shielded from any
more flashes, I checked myself out a little further.

Eight fingers capable of playing air guitar ✔

Two bendy thumbs ✔

Two movable feet complete with wiggly toes ✔

All were working. All felt normal. My ankles seemed OK
too. So did my knees and elbows. Sneakily, I squashed my
upper arms tight against my chest and checked out my

Himalayas. Even *they* felt fine and they've been freaking me out on a daily basis for at least a year.

So everything was OK then.

Good.

So why did everything feel so weird?

I slowly spread my fingers in front of my eyes and peered out through the gaps.

'Ronni . . . Just one little smile for the camera.'

On impulse, I moved my hands completely clear of my face, shook back my hair and pouted. My lip muscles felt normal too. And then it hit me.

Had someone just said camera?

My hands flew back to their original position faster than you can click SHARE. And, even though my body was frozen for a moment, my brain was suddenly working at a million miles per hour. And this time I wasn't thinking about my neck or my knees or my hips or my Himalayas – the only thing I was thinking was this:

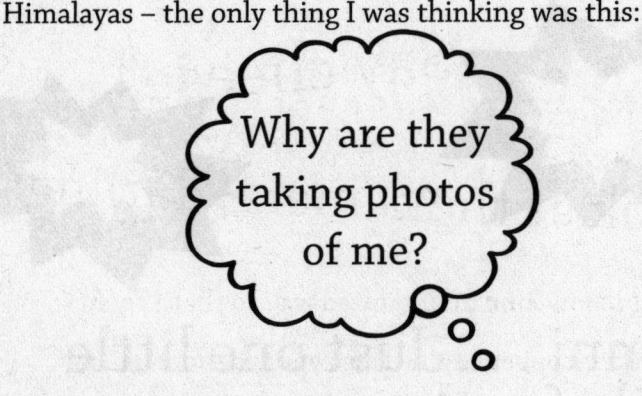

Why are they taking photos of me?

And who the heck were they anyway?

I breathed in. And I breathed out. And – very slowly – I spread my fingers once more.

And then I gasped.

In front of me was a mob of photographers. They were pressed together behind a length of gold-coloured rope and they were pushing and shoving and crushing in as closely as they could to get the best view of me. When

they spotted me peeping at them, they all opened up their mouths at once and shouted,

'Ronni!'

'This way, sweetheart.'

'Just one little smile.'

'Say cheese.'

'Look at the camera, darling.'

But not in any kind of organized way so that I could follow their conversation. This sounded more like my brothers shouting.

I blinked and snapped my fingers tight shut again. And then I whispered, 'Where in the world am I?'

Right next to me, a voice said, 'Here's a better question. What the heck did you do that for?'

It was a voice I recognized. Turning my head, I peeped out from behind my hands and saw Stuart Bolan sprawled on the ground next to me. He was rubbing his forehead

and looking annoyed. My eyes widened in surprise. I'd completely forgotten about him.

Stuart spotted me peeping. 'So? Why did you do it?'

I shook my head helplessly. And then, instead of even trying to answer his question, I asked him another. 'Why are all those people taking pictures of me?'

Stuart pushed his bottle-bleached fringe out of his face, rolled his eyes and said, 'Er . . . hello? *Zing!* Why d'you think?'

I shook my head again. And then I shrugged and said, 'I dunno.' And it was totally the truth. My brain was mush. It was like a wire had worked loose.

Stuart rolled his eyes a second time. 'You're Miss Ronni Runaway obviously! And thanks to that unscheduled somersault on the red carpet you're now going to be splashed over the front pages of every single newspaper in the world! And me with you! You've made us look like a right couple of jokers!'

Had he just said red carpet?

I froze.

And then I unfroze and looked down. Instead of the

dirty black floor of the dodgem track, I was sitting on a strip of soft red carpet. I shivered and looked upward. Instead of the low dark ceiling of Reggie Branning's undercover amusements, I could only see sky.

I looked at Stuart Bolan and said, 'Huh?'

Stuart was still rubbing his head. 'You didn't have to pull me down with you. That was just vinditious!' And then he flicked a V-sign at the photographers and muttered, 'Zing.'

I had no idea what he was talking about.

Above us, there was a loud cough. Another voice said, 'Yes. We are too long on red carpet. Get up, please.'

Stuart and I both looked up.

Standing over us – with his arms full of fresh flowers – was Yuri Maximovich Krolik. My jaw dropped open in astonishment. I'd completely forgotten about him as well. ~~To be fair, it's quite easily done because Yuri is quite tall and quite thin and quite quiet and quite ordinary-looking~~

Actually, I've crossed that last bit out because it simply wasn't true. There was no way anyone could miss Yuri Maximovich Krolik now. He looked like James Bond.

I stared at Yuri, flabbergasted. And then I said,

'What the heck are you wearing?'

Yuri looked down at his cream tuxedo. 'Yes, I have this suit made especially by very expensive tailor-man in Moscow. But now I am needing you to hurry up, please. This is potential bad situation. I don't want embarrassing media backslash.' And then he nodded his head at a big, bald, red-faced man in a black suit and said, 'Yes, please – you carry Ronni's flowers. They have damaging pollen which is ruining suit made by very expensive tailor-man in Moscow.'

The big, bald, red-faced man nodded back at Yuri and said, 'No problem, Mr Krolik,' and he stepped forward to take the flowers.

Still sitting on the red carpet, I stared up at Yuri and then I stared at the big, bald, red-faced man. And somewhere – in a slot machine deep inside my muddled brain – a penny dropped. I pointed a finger at the big, bald, red-faced man and said, 'But I saw you earlier! You're the Hopeless Henchman! What the heck are you doing here?

The Hopeless Henchman said, 'Steady on, Miss Runaway. I've never given you any reason to complain

about me so I can't be that hopeless!' And then he muttered, 'Flipping diva,' and walked over to the gold rope where some random maniac had pushed past all the photographers and was now trying to chuck roses at me.

You didn't have to be Seaside Sibyl to work out that something really wasn't right.

Yuri nodded impatiently. 'Yes yes. But of course you see him earlier. You see him many times. He is your bodyguard. But please not to call him Hopeless Henchman. This is total rudeness. His name is Dave.' Then he stooped down so that his face was close to mine, looked at me with a big worried frown and said, 'Yes but are you feeling OK, Ronni? You are acting like very strange abnormal person.'

Not for the first time, my jaw dropped. But then I remembered that Yuri's English isn't all that hot and closed it again.

Next to me, Stuart Bolan stopped looking thoroughly fed up and began to hoot with laughter. 'Oh, mate, just keep talking. You're flipping priceless,' he spluttered. And then he added, 'Oi, Spaceman, do something useful and help me up, will you? I've got

brand-new jeans on and my legs won't bend.'

Yuri pushed a strand of mousy hair away from his eyes, glanced coolly at Stuart and said, 'Yes but get up yourself. And, please, not to call me Spaceman. To you, I am Mr Krolik.' Then he turned back to me, took hold of both my hands and pulled me very quickly and very gently to my feet. It took me by surprise. As our hands joined, I couldn't help noticing how nice he smelt.

'Thanks,' I said, and suddenly felt a bit embarrassed. I'd never touched Yuri Maximovich Krolik before. He's not really one of those people you tend to touch.

Yuri nodded stiffly. 'Yes it is OK. You are welcome.'

'You smell well nice,' I said, and then I felt a lot embarrassed. I'd never smelt Yuri before either. He's not really one of those people you tend to sniff.

Yuri nodded stiffly again. 'Yes but I thank you. It is new manly fragrance by BCK.'

BCK? I'd never heard of it. But I smiled anyway and pretended I had.

Yuri lowered his voice, leaned in towards me and added, 'But this boyfriend of yours is a total loser, yes?'

Had he just said boyfriend?

I froze. Again.

And then I did something I definitely hadn't done for a while. I smiled.

Everyone fancies Stuart Bolan. It's a widely acknowledged fact that he's the coolest boy in town. Pope John Cool II and Coolius Caesar are lukewarm and undercooked next to him. If you want to know just how cool Stuart Bolan is, the situation is pretty much like this:

Stuart Bolan is the ice in your cola.

He's the air-conditioning in your Starbucks.

He's the calamine lotion on your chickenpox blister.

And as far as the girls in my school are concerned, Stuart Bolan is Daddy Cool. Even if he does smell of cigarettes.

So it's hardly any wonder that when Yuri used the word boyfriend, I felt ever so slightly giggly and dizzy and giddy and jiggly

and totally crazy like a fool.

I turned round to check out my boyfriend.

Stuart Bolan was back on his feet and sulkily brushing non-existent dust off his jeans.

I frowned.

It's no secret that Stuart Bolan only **ever** wears jeans. Everybody knows this. Even the teachers. But the jeans that Stuart wears are almost always skinny grey ones. Or occasionally skinny faded blue ones. And before the dodgem crash I'm sure he'd been wearing the grey variety. But now he was wearing a completely different pair altogether. They were big and baggy and dark and jeans-coloured and had bright gold stitching. And, while I was watching, Stuart staggered to his feet and turned away from me and, straight away, I saw there was a swirly design of sparkly little stones all over his back pockets. And across his bum were more sparkly little stones arranged like this:

I eyed Stuart Bolan's sparkly bum with growing suspicion.

StuBo?

I must have said it out loud. Stuart stopped brushing away non-existent dust and turned round. 'Yeah, babe,' he said. 'They're a limited edition of one by BCK. Made especially for me. Sweet or what?'

And instead of saying, 'Yeah, *StuBo*, they're sweet,' or, 'No, *StuBo*, they're utterly rancid,' I just said nothing at all and basked in the fact that

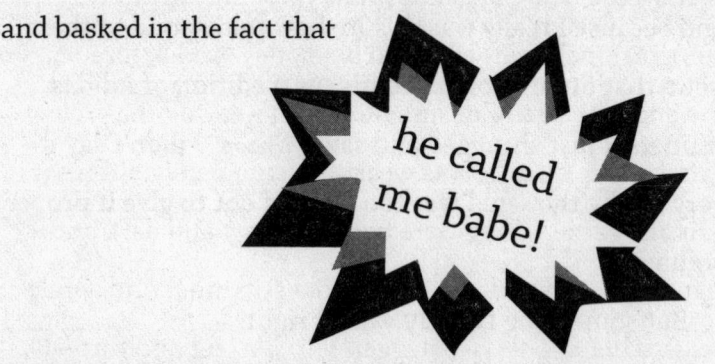

he called me babe!

And then I frowned. What was this BCK everyone was on about?

This time I must have kept my question to myself because Stuart just carried on talking. 'Mind you, babe, if you think my jeans are tasty, have a cheeky look at these. They are well nice.' And he kicked a foot forward so I could see his trainer. To be fair, it was quite impressive. It was gold and black and not like any other

trainer I've ever seen in the high street.

'Wow,' I said. 'Did you have to go all the way to Ipswich to get those?'

Stuart laughed. 'Ipswich? These have travelled further than that! They're direct from the Adidas design studio in Tokyo. They're called StuBos. They've got a picture of my face on the tongues.'

And because this entire situation was beyond weird and because I really wasn't sure how to respond to the news that Stuart Bolan had his own edition of Adidas trainers, I just shrugged and said, 'Whoop!' I didn't say it very loudly though. I was too freaked out to give it proper volume.

But something totally wasn't right.

Behind the gold rope at the edge of the red carpet, there was a commotion and the photographers all surged forward and began pushing and shoving again. One of them shouted, 'Look sharp, lads. Beyoncé and Jay-Z are here!'

And another one shouted, 'Get your cameras ready, boys.'

And another one shouted,

'They've got that geezer from Coldplay with them.'

And another one shouted,

'Ronni, darling, can you shift out of the way.'

Yuri Krolik's face grew more anxious. 'Yes but come. We are much too long on red carpet. It could be very bad situation. I am not wanting to have fight with Beyoncé. Hurry, please.' And grabbing Stuart and me both by an arm, he began marching us forward.

My feet fell into step. They were too freaked out to disobey. But as I marched my eyes were skipping about everywhere.

This was all so weird.

So **very** weird.

Looking ahead, I saw that the red carpet stretched the entire length of a long walkway before stopping in front of a pair of enormous doors. I glanced left and right.

Beyond the red carpet I could see more photographers and more crowds of cheering people. And beyond all of them, I could see . . . well, nothing.

Just sky.

Too much sky.

It was almost like we were marching straight through it.

A seagull screeched, swooped down and perched for a moment on the gold rope that separated us from everyone else. It put its head on one side and had a good look at me. Then it shook out its tail feathers, crapped out half its body weight in sloppy white bird poo and flew off again.

My feet stopped marching.

Yuri said, 'Keep moving, please. It is bad idea to keep Beyoncé waiting.'

My feet began to move again. Hurrying to keep up with the punishing pace of Yuri, I said, 'Is she really here? Beyoncé I mean. Is Beyoncé actually seriously here?'

Yuri Maximovich Krolik kept walking and said, 'Yes but of course.'

I trotted along next to him and tried to take this in. It

was hard. Beyoncé is one of the most famous people on the planet and I'm Ronni Runnacles. We don't tend to hang out in the same places. Also, it's extremely difficult to trot when your feet are absolutely killing you. I looked down and saw I was wearing a pair of gold boots with massive high heels. They weren't designed for trotting. They weren't even designed for walking. No wonder I'd somersaulted on the red carpet.

Or had I?

Wasn't there a dodgem involved somewhere?

Suddenly everything seemed way too complicated. So I gave up trying to work it all out and blurted out the one thing I really should have asked in the first place.

'Will somebody *please* just tell me where I am!'

Yuri stopped dead.

Stuart Bolan started laughing again and said, 'Babe, you are soooo random! Biggest night of your life and you don't even know where you are? You are one serious freak!' And then he stopped laughing and said, 'It was a joke, babe, yeah?'

Yuri peered at me with his anxious grey eyes and said,

'Yes but I knew it! I knew you are acting like strange abnormal person. You have bump on head. It make you sick. Tonight could be potential embarrassment with terrible media backslash.' And then he looked so anxious and so freaked out that – for a second – I actually stopped worrying about what the heck was happening to me and started worrying about Yuri instead.

'I'm OK,' I lied. 'I just want to know where I am. Because, wherever it is, it's not the place I was expecting to be right now.'

Stuart Bolan had been trying to contain his laughter, but when I said this he gave up and lost the battle. A little ripple of laughter spilt out of him. Then another. And another. They were like little laughter aftershocks.

Yuri shot him down with an irritated glance and then turned back to me. 'Ronni,' he said, 'you must remember. You are about to enter world-famous Copper Bowl for most important night in music-industry social calendar. How can you forget this? Tonight, you are guest of honour at Brit Award ceremony.'

Ronni Runnacles @ronneee_r

You're never more than six links
away from Madonna.

Or Prince Harry. Or the Pope. Or David Beckham. That's what the experts reckon anyway.

According to them, everybody in the entire world is connected in some way by a chain of no more than six links. These six links are called the Six Degrees of Separation. My nan once told me all about it. It works like this:

You know somebody who knows somebody who knows somebody who knows somebody who knows somebody who knows Madonna.

Although it doesn't have to be Madonna. It could be Prince Harry. Or the Pope. Or David Beckham. Or anyone else you like.

But this chain of connections doesn't include the internet. If it did, we wouldn't need so many links. In fact, we probably wouldn't need any links at all. We could probably just say something like

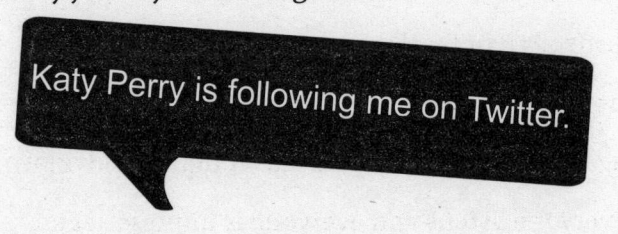

Katy Perry is following me on Twitter.

And we'd be straight there.

Bingo Bango!

Except we'd probably be lying. Or just talking about some random Katy Perry who works in Argos.

But, even without the internet, the world does seem to be getting smaller and the superstars are getting closer. For some people at least. My friend Flooky actually *is* only six degrees of separation away from Madonna. It works like this:

Flooky knows her mum who knows Janice Beany who knows Lesley Sweatbanks who knows Shirley Gammon who has a daughter called Mandy. Mandy works in a hairdressing salon in Ipswich. But, ages ago, she had a really interesting life and once blowdried Madonna's hair on the film set of *Evita*.

And that's fantastic for Flooky. She gets a lot of mileage out of that story. She tells it again and again and everyone listens and everyone is impressed and everyone asks her if she's ever met Shirley Gammon's

interesting daughter Mandy and if she knows whether Mandy managed to steal a strand of genuine Madonna hair.

But here's where the theory falls down. I've tried and tried and I can't link myself to Madonna at all. Not unless I tag myself on to the story that Flooky has already told. And there's no point doing that because who wants to listen? Seven degrees of separation isn't interesting. And, besides, there's nobody I could tell who wouldn't have already heard it from Flooky.

And I can't link myself to Prince Harry either. Or the Pope. Or David Beckham.

In fact – until yesterday – the best chain that I could come up with was this:

I know my nan who knows Bouncy Castle Ken who has a brother called Trevor who has a grandson called Kyle who plays football with a boy called Oscar who is the son of Daryl Onions who does the weather on *BBC Look East*.

Big whoop!

Over time, I've sort of accepted the fact that people like me in towns like mine are not all linked by six

degrees of separation to everyone else in the world.

We are cut off and on our own.

And I thought this meant that I would **never** meet anyone interesting. Or even **anyone** else who had once met **someone** who'd met **someone** who'd met **someone** who'd met **someone** who'd met **someone** interesting. And I **don't** mean Daryl Onions. Because people like me from towns like mine do not have those sort of thrilling encounters. Not unless your name is Flooky. And Flooky is already a lot more interesting than most people around here because:

a) her dad is Dutch

and

b) he owns loads of houses

and

c) nobody knows how to say her name properly.

But yesterday something changed.

Somehow, I somersaulted into another situation. And in this new situation I went from being six degrees of separation from Daryl Onions to being SLAP BANG WALLOP next to Beyoncé. And Jay-Z. And that man from Coldplay. And loads of other

massively interesting people too.

And the best thing about it was that they were all massively excited about being SLAP BANG WALLOP next to me!

And even though I still wasn't sure what the heck was going on, I started to relax a tiny bit. Because, whatever it was, it was a whole heap better than my normal situation – the one where I'm sitting in school and being moaned at by Mrs Booley or Dobby. Or I'm at home and listening to my four brothers shouting and crying and burping and farting. Or else I'm trying not to listen to the sound of my mum crying. Or I'm walking around feeling massively angry with my dad. Or I'm just secretly and silently missing him.

It was definitely better than all of that.

In fact – to begin with – this whole weird state of affairs was just like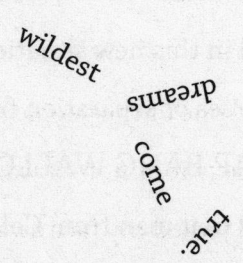

I was inside a massive indoor arena. It was heaving.
A few lucky people were sitting at shiny black tables
and looking beautiful, but most were on their feet and
looking fairly sweaty. Some of these sweaty sorts were
weaving between the tables with trays of drinks balanced
expertly on their fingertips. Others were rushing around
and shouting into headsets. Loads more were wandering
about and snapping away with enormous cameras. Mixed
in with the general hum of chattering and cheering and
laughter and music, I could hear

Snap.

Snap.

Snap.

Snap.

Snap.

And one of the people being snapped at was me. Because –
believe it or not – *I* was one of the beautiful ones.

I jerked my face away from the flash of a camera and

looked up. In front of me was a massive stage. But apart from a few more of those sweaty sorts wearing headsets nobody was on it yet.

I looked over my shoulder. Behind me were more tables with more people sitting around them and more waiters weaving their way past more flashing photographers. And behind them all was

asolidwallofpeople

that rose right up into the roof of the arena. I'd never seen so many people. It was like I'd suddenly barged my way into the middle of Madonna's world tour or bagged the very best seat at the Olympics.

Then I looked back at my table. Including me, there were six people sitting round it. On my left, Yuri Maximovich Krolik was ignoring everything and reading a thick paperback book. I doubt most people would bother taking a book to the Brit Awards, but Yuri Maximovich Krolik isn't like most people.

On my right, Stuart Bolan had his feet up and was shouting into the ear of Dave the Bodyguard. Even though the arena was so noisy I could hardly hear myself

think, I knew Stuart was talking about his Adidas StuBos. Above the chat and the cheers and the laughs and the snaps and the background music, I heard him bellow, 'They've got a picture of my face on the tongues.'

On the other side of the table were two old ladies I didn't know.

Or did I?

I looked at them again. They both looked weirdly familiar. Sort of like my nan but far cooler. Instead of my nan's spiky copper hair, one of them had a silver crop and the other was wearing a stylish black beret. She'd teamed the beret with a shiny orange dress so that she looked a bit like a funky wasp. Both of the old ladies had immaculately shaped eyebrows.

They smiled at me so I automatically smiled back. Then, the one with the silver skinhead leaned across the table and said loudly, 'Are you OK, Ronni? Is there anything you need?'

And I automatically replied, 'I think so. I don't think so.'

It seemed like a perfectly reasonable response, but both the old ladies looked at me and frowned. So did

Yuri. Suddenly shutting his book, he said, 'Yes but I cannot concentrate on intense Russian novel. I am distracted by worrying situation. I think that Ronni is not feeling right in head.'

'My head is fine,' I snapped.

The old lady with the crop said, 'Well, we're here if . . .' But then she paused. The arena had gone weirdly quiet. It was like those random moments we sometimes get in food technology when everyone's cake-mixing arms are badly aching and we're way too weak to speak. But this was on a much bigger scale. The skinhead lady adjusted her volume and started again. 'Well, we're here if you do need something, Ronni. So tell us. Don't just sit there like a lemon. We'll get you anything you need. That's our job. We're your entourage.'

'Oh,' I said – and sat there like a lemon for a few seconds while I thought about this. And then I said, 'I need a Knickerbocker Glory.'

The weirdly quiet moment passed. The chatter and cheering and laughter returned to full power. Crossing my fingers beneath the table, I watched as the closely cropped old lady pulled a walkie-talkie from her pocket,

put it to her lips and shouted, 'I need a Knickerbocker Glory for Miss Ronni Runaway. As quick as you can.'

Stuart Bolan took his mouth away from Dave the Bodyguard's ear and said, 'Sue, make that two. I'll have one as well.'

Skinhead Sue raised the walkie-talkie again and bellowed, 'Make that two. StuBo wants one as well.'

I uncrossed my fingers and sat there astonished. This was not a familiar situation.

'Actually,' I shouted, 'I think I might need a glass of pink champagne as well.'

'And me,' chipped in Stuart.

'With a cherry in,' I shouted.

'And me,' chipped in Stuart.

Instead of laughing in my face and telling me I could choose between a glass of orange squash or nothing, Sue just nodded. I watched in delighted disbelief as she raised her walkie-talkie yet again so that she could bark my order to the bar.

But then the wasp woman sprang up from her seat and

said, 'Wait. I'll get it. It's my turn!'

Sue lowered her walkie-talkie and shrugged.

Mrs Wasp buzzed over to my side of the table and said, 'I'll get it myself. It'll be just as quick. And I'll listen out for any word on who might win Best British Female Artist.' And then she winked at me before buzzing off to find me fizzy pink champagne.

I sat back in my seat and said one word.

'Whoop.'

I meant it as well. Because if that's not the precise moment in life to say 'whoop' I really don't know when is.

I looked at Yuri. And then I put my mouth very close to his ear and said, 'Will those two old ladies get me anything?'

Behind us there was a roar. We both turned round. The people in the cheap seats were doing a Mexican wave.

Yuri frowned at them. Then he frowned at me and said, 'Yes but no. I am your manager so I am making

final decision. And I cannot risk repeat of embarrassing situation like the London Olympics opening ceremony.'

My mouth dropped open. And then I tapped my ears, shook my head and said, 'Sorry? Say that again?'

'Yes. The London Olympics opening ceremony,' said Yuri. 'Surely you can remember this?' And then he sighed and added, 'Yes but you probably cannot. You drank very much champagne and became sick just before you were supposed to sing important song at very important moment. If this nice person, Emeli Sandé, had not stepped in and sung instead, there would have been total London Olympic disaster.'

It's hard to know how to respond to a piece of information like this. So I didn't say anything.

Yuri gave me a firm look. 'Yes. So tonight you have one small glass only.'

A waiter arrived with my Knickerbocker Glory and placed it on the table in front of me. It was in a glass so tall that my nan would have stuck daffodils in it. The ice cream was swimming in a sea of hot fudge sauce and almost buried beneath fluffy pink and white marshmallows. I've lived my whole life in a town full of

ice-cream kiosks, but the scale of this ice cream was a completely new experience.

'Whoop,' I said, and picked up my spoon.

Sue snapped her fingers at the waiter and said, 'You need to sharpen up your act, sunshine. We've been waiting over *two minutes*. You can't expect to keep a star like Miss Ronni Runaway waiting. It's just not on.'

The waiter mouthed the words, 'Sorry, madam.' And then he looked at me, turned bright red and mouthed, 'Sorry, madam,' to me too. And then he bowed.

Mrs Wasp returned with an ice bucket and an entire bottle of pink champagne. 'I'm sorry I was ages,' she shouted. 'This place is mayhem.'

'It's OK,' I said, and stuffed a big spoonful of ice cream, fudge sauce and marshmallow into my mouth.

And it was OK.

In fact, it was better than OK. And even though there were thousands of people doing a Mexican wave a couple of hundred metres behind my back I was feeling less and less freaked out, and more and more relaxed. And, anyway, what was the point of worrying about some

stupid little somersault on a dodgem track? Or a red
carpet? Or wherever it was that I'd bumped my head . . .

A smile crept over my face.

In front of me was:

• the biggest Knickerbocker Glory I'd ever seen in my
    entire life

• a glass of pink champagne with a cherry in it

• two old ladies who were falling over themselves to get
    me whatever I wanted

• a manager

• a bodyguard, and

• a boyfriend everyone thought was cooler than the ice
    in my champagne bucket.

The Wasp was wrong. This wasn't mayhem. This was
paradise.

I looked to my left and checked out a little more of it.

On the next table – in close conversation with Sir Paul
McCartney – was Lady Gaga.

I looked to my right.

Beyoncé, Jay-Z and that man from Coldplay were
busily tucking into a bowl of cheesy footballs.

Yes. I said *Beyoncé*.

Not Kelly Rowland. Not Michelle Williams. This was the actual

living

breathing

walking

talking

singing

posing

dancing

pouting

strutting

sparkling female

human being who goes by the name of Beyoncé Giselle

Knowles-Carter. And she was just a few metres away from me. And Sir Paul McCartney, Lady Gaga, Jay-Z and that man from Coldplay were just a few metres away from me too. And I wasn't hearing about this from somebody who knew somebody who knew somebody who knew somebody who knew somebody who once sat in a room with these people. No. I. Wasn't.

Because this time that somebody in the room was me!

'Whoop,' I said. 'It's like I've died and gone to Heaven.' And, automatically, my hand searched for my phone so that I could tell my seven followers about this in no more than 140 characters. But then I remembered that I didn't have a phone – and that this was actually no bad thing because I didn't have any pockets either. Just gold high-heeled boots, a matching gold jacket and shorts so short that my nan would have spat out her soft mints.

'You haven't died,' said Yuri, firmly. 'You just have bump on head. And you are not in Heaven. You are in the Copper Bowl on the Pier, obviously!'

I stared at him.

The Copper Bowl on the Pier?

My brain dropped into my stomach.

My stomach dropped down to my ankles.

For a second, I sat as still as a lemon and thought about what Yuri had just said. And then I curled my hand into a tight fist and dug my fingernails as hard as I could into my palms.

It hurt.

Satisfied, I took hold of Yuri's arm and said, 'Did I just hear that right? Did you just say the Copper Bowl on the Pier?'

'Yes,' said Yuri.

My brain slipped down to my knees. My stomach slid down to my toes. I looked around. This was the glitziest, swankiest and most razzle-dazzle place I'd ever seen. Even without the presence of Beyoncé and co.

'Copper Bowl?' I said.

'Yes,' said Yuri.

'On the *Pier*?'

'Yes.'

I glanced around again. There wasn't a Burnout game or a one-armed bandit or a fortune-telling gumball machine in sight.

'Ohmigod, this is way too weird! I've got to get out,' I said, and sprang to my feet.

Yuri Krolik sprang up too. 'Where are you going? You must take bodyguard with you.'

There was a snap and a flash and someone else said,

'Ronni, can we just have one little smile for *The New York Times*?'

Ignoring them both, I raised my arm in front of my face and rushed off towards the nearest EXIT sign. I had to get outside. I needed fresh air. Desperately. And for all the helpfulness of the two old women in my entourage, I was pretty sure that this was one thing I had to get for myself.

Somewhere behind me, I heard voices calling my name. I moved faster. Paradise or not, I had to get out. I needed to sort everything out in my mind.

I looked up and saw the exit was right in front of me. I put my head down again and rushed towards it and

'Ouch,' I said.

The unexpected obstacle said, 'Sorry, madam.'

It was a woman. She was SLAP BANG WALLOP between me and the way out. She wasn't taking photographs or rushing around with a tray in her hand – she was just standing there. And whereas everyone else was dressed in sparkly jackets and sparkly boots and

specially commissioned jeans and limited-edition trainers and BCK designer wear – whatever *that* was – and glittery dresses and tight shiny suits, she was dressed in proper trousers and proper shoes and a bright yellow jacket.

Somewhere in my muddled brain, a penny dropped.

'Oh my God,' I said. 'You're that flipping truancy officer, aren't you?'

The woman gave me a funny look. 'No, madam,' she said. 'I'm Security.' And then she turned round so that I could see the word printed on the back of her jacket: SECURITY.

'Oh,' I said. 'But you look exactly like the truancy officer who was hanging around here earlier.' And then I frowned and added, 'Well, not here exactly. Not how it is now anyway. I'm talking about before – when it was all just slot machines.'

The security woman gave me another funny look.

'I really need some fresh air,' I said.

The security woman said, 'I think you're probably right,' and stepped aside.

As soon as I was past her, I ran through the doorway, legged it up a corridor, flew down a flight of steps, legged

it down another corridor and darted through another door. And finally – to my relief – I found myself outside and alone. More or less alone anyway. Some distance away on a long low wall, I could see a few people sitting very quietly and very still. *I* stood very still too and took a few deep breaths. Wherever this place was, it didn't feel like it belonged in the same universe as the chaos of the red carpet. I must have come out via a back door.

I waited until I'd got my breath back and then I had a proper look around.

I was standing on a vast paved terrace in the shadow of the enormous white arena. Set into the paving stones – every few steps – was a gold star. I looked at the one closest to my feet. It said Beyoncé. I looked at another. It said Brad Pitt. I scratched my head. And then I began to follow the path of the stars at my feet and I read the names as I went.

LADY
GAGA

CHRIS
MARTIN

I paused. And then I frowned and muttered, 'Who the heck is he?'

I scratched my head and looked up. Beyond the low walls of the terrace – which were now a whole lot closer – I could see the sea. Miles and miles of it. And it was a sea I recognized. Even in the fading daylight, it was sparkling and shimmering and shining and twinkling and looking ever so slightly like it might be some sort of greyish brown shade of blue.

'But this can't be the Copper Bowl on the Pier,' I said out loud to nobody. 'It's blatantly impossible.'

One of the people sitting on the low wall at the edge of the terrace said, 'Oi, I don't care how famous you are – keep the bloody noise down. You'll frighten the fish away.'

I looked at the row of grumpy fisherman in front of me. And then I whispered, 'Oh my God.'

Behind me, there was a commotion, and the door I'd escaped from a little earlier burst open. Yuri Maximovich Krolik, Dave the Bodyguard, the old woman called Sue and the other old woman who looked like a wasp came running across the terrace towards me. To be fair, those two old ladies could shift.

The grumpiest fisherman on the wall said, 'Flipping Nora! I've had enough of this. It's like Trafalgar Square around here. I'm packing up and going home.' And he began reeling his fishing line in.

Yuri lurched to a halt in front of me. 'Yes. There you are! I am feeling big sensations of relief.'

Dave the Bodyguard was only a couple of paces behind him. He shook his head, looked at me sternly and said, 'Don't go wandering off again. Anything could've happened. You're a superstar, Ronni, and it's my job to keep you safe. I'm your perfect bodyguard.'

The two old ladies pulled up, huffing and puffing. Sue said, 'You should've asked us if you needed something.'

And Mrs Wasp said, 'That's what we're here for. We're your entourage.'

I looked at them all. And then I said, 'Where's Stuart? He should be here. He's supposed to be my boyfriend, isn't he?'

'Yes but he is idiot,' said Yuri.

I almost argued back, but then I let it go. There was way too much other stuff on my mind. 'I just don't get it,' I said. 'How can I be Miss Ronni Runaway? I'm not! I'm *really* not! I'm just stupid boring Veronica Runnacles. That's who I *am*. I don't even have a middle name!'

Yuri looked surprised. Then he shook his head very firmly and said, 'Yes but this is not true. You have never been stupid boring Veronica Runnacle. How can think this?'

For a second I just stared at him. Then I lowered my gaze and shook my head too, but there was nothing firm about my headshake. Mine was the saddest and flakiest and most confused and most freaked out and most hopeless expression of total frustration that there has probably ever been.

But I still had questions.

Lots of them.

I took a deep breath and said, 'How can *I* be at the Brit Awards? In this massive swanky arena? How is that *even possible*? A couple of hours ago, I was here playing Burnout and having my tea leaves read!'

Sue nodded sympathetically. 'That's right, love. You are burnt out. All these tours and parties and award ceremonies are taking their toll. You're only a young'un, after all. But there's no chance of a break yet. Not with your schedule.'

And Mrs Wasp said, 'If there's anything we can do to make life easier, Ronni, just ask. Don't sit and stew like a casserole.'

The edges of Yuri's eyes crinkled with concern. 'Yes but this is bad. Very, very bad. I think you are mentally altered by bump on head.'

More confused than ever, I raised a hand and rubbed the sore spot on my crown. *Was I really Miss Ronni Runaway?*

'I just can't believe this,' I said. 'It's too, too weird. Things like this just don't happen to people like me. I'm nobody.'

'You are **not** nobody,' said Yuri. And he pointed down at the ground. 'Look.'

I looked. And there it was. Sunk into a paving slab just a metre or so away from my feet.

MISS RONNI
RUNAWAY

And I had no idea who'd put it there.

Or when.

Or why.

And I had no idea what pier I was on or what channel I was watching or even what planet I inhabited.

But I was suddenly certain of something.

This weird world I'd somersaulted into was heaps cooler and heaps more interesting than the one I'd woken up in this morning.

I stared down at my star and then – eventually – I looked up at my manager and my bodyguard and my entourage. A tiny smile was making my lips twitch. And

the tiny smile grew into a bigger and bigger smile and – within just a second or two – my cheeks were actually hurting because I was smiling so hard.

'We'd better go back in,' I said. 'I want to find out who wins Best British Female Artist.'

Ronni Runnacles @ronneee_r

It's not about taking part, it's about winning.

That's what I've always believed anyway. Because if I didn't think I could win, I wouldn't bother taking part in the first place.

And that leaves me in a bit of a difficult position because, the truth is I've never won anything.

And I mean never.

In my whole life, I've won a grand total of nothing.

Nada.

Zilch.

Not a sausage.

Diddly squat.

I've never even won a crappy consolation prize.

And every single time I've failed to grab a teddy with an electronic claw or missed the coconut on the coconut shy or finished seventh in a sack race or fifty-ninth in a spelling competition or not had a winning ticket or never heard back from the organizers or been told by Piers Morgan that I'm rubbish, my nan or my mum or some other wise person has said, 'Never mind, Ronni, it's the taking part that counts. Maybe you'll win next time.'

And, instead of believing them, I've always abandoned hope, dropped my chin, slumped my shoulders and thought

Big. Fat. Whoop!

But yesterday, in this bizarre new world of the Copper Bowl on the Pier, the possibility of failure didn't even enter my head. Instead, I lifted my chin, straightened my back and let my confidence soar as high as a seagull. This was finally going to be my time to win.

By the time I got back to my table, the ceremony was just about to begin. Everyone had topped up their glasses, the photographers had been told to sit down, Sir Paul McCartney and Lady Gaga were no longer in deep conversation and Beyoncé, Jay-Z and that man from Coldplay were wiping cheesy crumbs off their chops and staring eagerly at the stage. The atmosphere in the arena was awesome for suresome.

The people crowded into the stands behind us were waving their arms like Mexicans and others were holding up their phones and taking photos and my ears were ringing with the sound of thousands and thousands of people clapping their hands and stamping their feet and screaming and shrieking and laughing and cheering and chanting . . .

'Ronni!
Ronni!
Ronni!'

'They're shouting my name,' I said in amazement.

'Of course they are, babe,' shouted Stuart. 'They love you. You're cooler than the Great Cool of China. You're even cooler than me.'

My amazement doubled.

Stuart snorted into his pink champagne and said, 'Joke.'

A bolt of irritation shot through me. But then I laughed. There were thousands and thousands of people chanting *my* name. What was the point of feeling irritated at a moment like that?

I pulled a face at Stuart and turned to Yuri. 'Do you think I could win?'

Frowning, Yuri put down his book. After a long pause, he said, 'Yes. You have very good year. You have seven hit singles, plus Number One-selling album in fifty-nine different countries plus very high-profile legal battle with Piers Morgan. General public are liking you a lot.'

'Whoop,' I said.

'Oh, and I almost forgot,' added Yuri, 'you also won a Golden Globe award for writing and singing the theme tune for *Moonfinger*.'

I stared at him blankly. '*Moonfinger*?'

'Yes.' Yuri nodded. 'Most successful James Bond movie *ever*.'

My blankness was washed away by a massive wave of pride.

'Whoop,' I said again. And I meant it. I was amazing!

Yuri's eyes lingered on mine. Then he frowned again and put his mouth so close to my ear that it tickled. 'Yes,' he said. 'But it is idiot who counts eggs before they become chickens. You have very stiff competition.'

'Like who?' I pulled my ear away and glanced around at the other tables. Then I put my mouth to *his* ear and said, 'Not Beyoncé because she isn't British. And the same goes for Lady Gaga. So *who* can possibly beat me?' And I gulped down the last drop of my pink champagne, lifted my chin up very high and said, 'Don't you know who I am? I'm Miss Ronni Runaway!'

Yuri said, 'Yes but . . .'

'Trust me,' I said. 'This is my time!'

And it was as well! I knew it. I could feel it in every atom of my body. How could it not be my time? I'd been dreaming about stuff like this for the past month! I'd been dreaming that there was something more to my life than mooching about on my own and feeling fed up and miserable. And now I was actually living the dream

and there was no way I was going to fail or miss or screw things up. I was going to win. Because it was my moment to win. At last, I was going to be able to stand up in front of the whole world and say . . .

Thank you so much. Thank you for giving me this award. It means such a lot to know that I'm surrounded by so many amazing fans who love my music and respect my style and value my tireless efforts to be a positive influence on young people all over the world. I couldn't have done any of this without your incredible support. Because, as you know, I've been through some tough times. Real tough times! For a while, my family situation was a flipping nightmare. But thanks to my extraordinary and unique talent, I had the opportunity to escape all that. And I snatched that opportunity with both hands. And now I'm a celebrity. And somebody special. And the kind of person who stands out from the pack. So thank you all for making me your winner this evening. Good night and God bless.

And everyone was going to rise to their feet in a spontaneous standing ovation and they'd clap their hands until they were red and aching, and Beyoncé and Lady Gaga would be on their feet and clapping too, and tears of love and sisterhood would be streaming freely down their beautiful cheeks.

I could see all this as clearly as if it was happening.

But the picture was shrinking. And then – from some dark corner of my brain – Seaside Sibyl barged her way forward and began to grow.

My eyes widened in surprise. 'What are you doing here?'

Seaside Sibyl said something, but I couldn't hear what it was. All I could see was her mouth moving. I squinted at her and stared into the black hole in my head.

But I still couldn't understand. I felt my spirits sink. I'd completely forgotten about Seaside Sibyl. In fact, I'd

completely forgotten about a lot of people. Everything before the red carpet seemed really hazy and distant and grey and boring. Everything before the red carpet seemed pointless.

So I scrubbed Sibyl from my mind, picked up the bottle of pink fizz in front of me and began to pour myself another drink.

'Yes but I am here because I am manager,' said Yuri, who was frowning harder than ever. Placing his hand over the top of my super-skinny champagne glass, he added, 'And you must have no more of this. Anyway, ceremony is now starting.'

I puffed out my cheeks, put the bottle of pink fizz down again and looked up at the stage. And what I saw made me instantly stop sulking. What I saw made me feel as if I was totally weightless and floating

among

the

stars.

The gigantic stage of the Copper

Bowl on the Pier was a dazzling

spectacle of swirling lights and

riotous colours and sharp haircuts

and pouting faces and flawless...

...dance moves and buzzing guitars

and thumping drums and the plink

plink plink of electronic keyboards

and a mash-up of songs and a

clash of egos and...

...speeches filled with gratitude

and the occasional explosion of

attitude and a million more

moments of pure pop bliss.

In fact, it was amazing.

I suppose.

I'm sure I'd have thought so if I'd been sitting at home watching it all on my telly, anyway.

But when you're a star yourself and floating weightlessly and effortlessly among other stars, it's actually not quite as spectacular and amazing as you'd expect, because you quickly start to get used to the situation. Before you know it, you're looking at each new star who arrives on stage and making silent judgements and comparisons and criticisms in your head. And after a while, those dazzling A-listers stop looking so sparkly and amazing and start looking more like this:

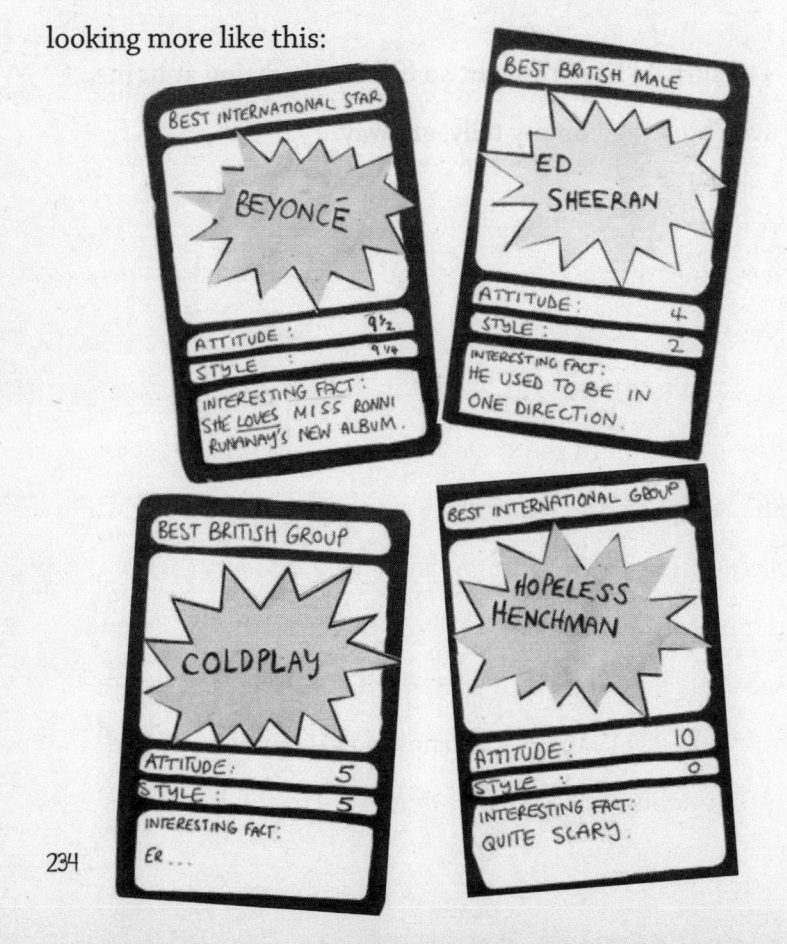

So I sat on the edge of my seat and waited for the only moment of pop bliss which *really* mattered. And, at last, an invisible Geordie announcer boomed, 'And now to present the award for Best British Female Artist, please welcome on to the stage Dobinella Dobinelli.'

The audience burst into applause. I sat even further forward in my seat and whispered, 'Who the heck is Dobinella Dobinelli?'

Stuart Bolan looked my way and raised his eyebrows. In a loud whisper back to me, he said, 'Dobinella Dobinelli? The world's greatest fashion designer? She's even cooler than BCK! Don't you know anything, Runny Nose?'

'Don't call me Ru –' And then I stopped. A woman had walked on to the stage carrying a large gold envelope. She was quite small and quite thin and wearing a big hand-knitted stripy jumper and baggy leggings that flapped around her ankles. Even from a distance, I could see that she was wearing two totally different socks.

'Oh my God,' I shouted. 'It's Dobby!'

But nobody else seemed shocked. They didn't even

seem surprised. Not even Stuart Bolan – and hadn't he been on the receiving end of one of her boring job leaflets just a few hours earlier?

I nudged him and whispered, 'What's she doing here?'

Stuart said, 'Didn't you just hear? She's about to give you your award.'

I smiled. Even in a severe state of Dobby-Shock, it was impossible not to.

Stuart gazed at the stage admiringly and said, 'That woman has a style which is totally her own.'

I'd never thought about it like that before.

Dobinella Dobinelli pulled a tissue out from her sleeve, rubbed her nose vigorously and then put the tissue back again. Leaning forward so that her mouth was practically touching the microphone, she said, 'I'm so honoured to be giving this award to a young woman who has *always* believed in doing her own thing . . .'

I smiled again.

'. . . And so it gives me great pleasure to announce that the award for Best British Female Artist goes to . . .'

Dobinella paused.

I checked out the route from my seat to the stage to make sure it was clear.

Dobinella still paused.

I ran my fingers over my eyebrows to check that I wasn't doing an impression of Ming the Merciless.

Dobinella still paused. *Oh, get on with it*, I thought.

Dobinella smiled, looked straight towards me and said, 'Sadie Slow Groove!'

I stood up.

And then I collapsed back into my seat again.

Sa—

Sa—

Words were failing me. Even inside my head. Finally, my brain recovered enough to spell out

Sadie?

And then it switched to size 125 font and thundered,

Sadie Slow *Groove*?

My body and my belly and my brain went numb. I looked up at the stage. Dobby was still staring straight at me and now she was smiling widely and clapping. The cameramen were all looking in my direction too and so were the press photographers who had suddenly reappeared in swarms.

'Huh?' I said.

And then I realized something spectacularly awful. Dobby Dobinella Dobinelli wasn't looking straight at me. Actually, she was looking straight over my head and behind me. And all the photographers and cameramen were looking straight over my head and behind me too.

I whipped round.

Sadie Slowgrove – or should I call her Slow Groove? – was already on her feet and crying and kissing people. No wonder I hadn't spotted her earlier. She looked totally different to how I'd ever seen her before. She had her hair up in complicated little sausage-shaped curls and she was wearing a tight shiny bottle-green dress with a shimmering purple sash across it.

Stuart Bolan said, 'Wow. She looks well hot!'

And Yuri Maximovich Krolik said, 'Yes but she has had very good year too. She has eight hit singles, plus Number One-selling album in sixty different countries plus high-profile love affair with Prince Harry. Also she won Oscar for her movie role as Bond girl. I thought there was possibility she might win.'

And even though he was still talking I couldn't hear the rest of it because the same crowd who had chanted my name earlier began to shout,

'SADIE! SADIE! SADIE!'

I couldn't stand any more of it. Before I'd even had a chance to ask my brain for permission, I got up out of my seat, stared straight into the nearest TV camera and screamed,

'That stupid girl ruins everything!'

Ronni Runnacles @ronneee_r

Sometimes there's nothing left to say.
#sojustshutup

But Yuri Maximovich Krolik didn't shut up. He came straight out and said it.

'Yes, well you are idiot!'

I glared at him. And then I looked around the massive limousine and glared at everybody else too.

Furthest away and sitting in the driving seat was Dave the Perfect Bodyguard. But I could only see the back of his head. I stopped wasting my energy and glared at my entourage instead. They were perched at the far end of a long sideways sofa and had their eyes closed. Every so often, one of them would let out a big sleepy snort, blink furiously, scratch her Himalayas and then nod off to sleep again.

My glare of fury faded to a frown of disappointment. I surely had the most boring entourage in the entire world.

Next to them was Yuri Maximovich Krolik and next to Yuri was Stuart and next to Stuart was me. And I wasn't enjoying this limo ride anywhere near as much as I might have dreamed. In fact, I wasn't enjoying it at all.

I suppose the problem pretty much boiled down to this: instead of laughing and sipping bubbly and being whisked through the stylish streets of New York City,

I was sitting in a sulky strop, crunching on a soft mint and waiting for the traffic lights to change. Through the smoked glass windows, I could see a branch of Lidl.

Yuri swallowed hard, dug a bit of soft mint out of his teeth with his fingernail and said again, 'Yes. I say it again. I think you are very much idiot.'

I couldn't keep my mouth shut any longer. I leaned forward in my seat and said, 'Did I just hear that right? Did you just call me an idiot?' I don't know why I even bothered to ask. I already knew the answer.

'Yes,' said Yuri. 'You still have much to learn in ways of global superstar.'

I opened my mouth to say something else. And then I sighed and snapped it shut again. For a second, all I could hear was the low throb of the engine and the occasional snorts of my two old ladies. In silent exasperation, I turned away from the whole lot of them and peered out through the limo's window. On the wall next to the Lidl store was a massive billboard poster advertising BCK aftershave. I sighed again, gave Stuart a sharp nudge and said, 'Back me up, Stuart. You're supposed to be my boyfriend.'

Stuart flicked his fringe out of his face and said crossly, 'You've got to drop this Stuart thing. The name's StuBo. You wouldn't go calling Jay-Z *Stuart*, would you?'

'No, because it's not his—'

But before I could finish, StuBo raised his hand and placed one finger lightly on my lips. Then he shook his head and said, '*Zing!*'

My body broke out into a hot flush. I'm not sure if it was because Stuart Bolan's finger was touching my lips or because I was fighting a sudden strong urge to throw a bowl of cake mix at him.

Stuart lowered his finger and grinned like a Cheshire Cat. Then he sat back in his seat and said, 'The Spaceman does have a point though, babe. You were a bit of an idiot tonight. Sadie Slow Groove totally out-classed you.'

'Huh?' I waited for him to tell me he was joking.

He didn't.

'Well, thanks a bunch,' I said.

Still grinning, Stuart said, 'No worries. I say what I see.' He began to laugh. 'You should have seen your face when Sadie made her speech. You looked like you were sucking a snail!'

The hot flush returned. I didn't want to hear this. Not from Stuart Bolan. Not from anyone, in fact. Losing out to Sadie Slowgrove had been vile enough, but her acceptance speech had totally pushed me over the edge. I closed my eyes and saw the whole horrible scene all over again. Sadie had floated to the stage on a cloud of triumph, taken her trophy from Dobinella Dobinelli and said . . .

Thank you so much. Thank you for giving me this award. I couldn't have done any of this without your help. As you all know, I've been through some tough times. Real tough times! For a while, my family situation was a flipping nightmare. But I know I'm not the only one who has found life challenging. There's somebody else in this arena who went through those same tough times too. And, even though we haven't always seen eye to eye, I'd like her to know that I'm on her side. I really am. So thank you all for making me your winner but, tonight, I'm going to share this award with . . . Ronni Runaway. Good night and God bless.

And then – while all the audience were holding up their phones and taking photos or clapping their hands and stamping their feet and shouting and cheering and chanting Sadie's name, she'd looked straight at me, given me a great big laughing grin and silently said,

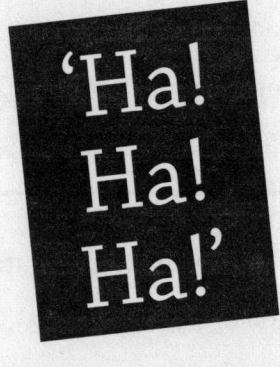

'Ha! Ha! Ha!'

And **that** was when I'd properly kicked off.

I opened my eyes and pushed the memory out of my head. It was too upsetting. Ignoring Stuart, I turned back to Yuri and snapped, 'So I'm an idiot! Did I even ask for your opinion?'

Yuri shook his head. 'Yes you didn't. But I tell you anyway.' And then he shrugged and added, 'But who knows? Maybe you'll win next time.'

Not for the first time, my mouth fell open. And not for the first time, it snapped shut again. If there'd been a mirror handy, I'd have probably mistaken myself for

a great big flappy-mouthed fish with ears. But I wasn't being deliberately fishy. There was just something about Yuri's logic which was tangling my head up into a topknot. After trying and failing to think of anything halfway decent to snap back at him with, I just gave up and said, 'Well, thank you for your input, Yuri. That was extremely helpful.'

Yuri gave me a stiff little smile. 'You are welcome.'

Far ahead through the distant windscreen, I saw the traffic lights change to amber and then green. The limo pulled forward. Both the old ladies snorted, blinked at us, yawned and shut their eyes again. And even though I was wound up tighter than a fishing reel, a yawn forced its way through my mouth too. Perhaps sleepiness is infectious. Or perhaps the truth is that I was just dog-tired.

Another yawn escaped. This one was so big it made my mouth open up as round as an American ring doughnut.

Actually, the truth is that I was more than dog-tired, I was exhausted. Not winning the award for Best British Female had been an emotionally draining business. And even though I'd got a massive buzz from being so

physically close to Beyoncé and Jay-Z and that man from Coldplay, the buzz was long gone. All I wanted now was to be by myself inside my bed inside my bedroom inside my home.

Home?

I jumped in my seat.

I'd forgotten about home. And I'd forgotten about my mum. In all the confusion and weirdness and excitement and disappointment, she'd sort of faded from my mind. I frowned. *Hadn't there been an argument at breakfast?*

My hands jerked into action and I patted my pockets to see if she'd left me any messages. And then I remembered. I had no pockets and I had no phone. My shoulders slumped. Without my phone, I didn't feel properly dressed. And I felt quite sad too. Sort of like I'd floated miles out to sea on a lilo and nobody knew I was even missing.

Biting my lip, I twisted in my seat again and pressed my face right up against the smoked-glass window. Outside, it was now dark and the street lights had come on. I put my thumbnail between my teeth and bit that

too. My mum would be worrying her head off. And as for my nan . . . I didn't even dare to think what she was going to say.

I turned back round. 'What time is it?'

Stuart didn't reply. He'd plugged himself into his iPod and closed his eyes. It was a relief, to be honest. Stuart's constant coolness gets a bit boring after a while.

Yuri Maximovich Krolik stroked his chin as if he was puzzling over something very, **very** complicated. Then, finally, he said, 'Yes. It's always teatime!'

I stared at him. Confused.

Yuri leaned forward, opened the door of a small cupboard built into the velvet interior of the limousine and pulled out a tea-making contraption. As I watched, he began to fiddle about with the buttons.

I stared at him. Still confused. And even though I would **never** say it, I was pretty much thinking this:

You are *such* a random freak sometimes.

But I kept it to myself because freak is a very harsh word. Even in these circumstances. So instead I just said, 'I don't want a cup of tea, Yuri. I want to go home.'

Yuri stopped fiddling with his tea-maker and shrugged. 'Yes. Of course. Driver will be reaching your penthouse apartment very soon.'

I stopped breathing.

My p—

My p—

My p—

Yuri looked anxious. 'Yes but are you OK? You appear to be experiencing air-supply problem.'

'Oh,' I said, and took a few deep and careful breaths. And then, when I'd recovered enough, I said, 'I'm sorry, Yuri, did you just say that I live in a penthouse apartment?'

'Yes,' said Yuri.

'Oh,' I said. And I stopped breathing again.

The limo drove on through the darkness. In the darkest darkness of my brain, there was now just one single thought:

I live in a *penthouse apartment?*

Individually these six words were fine. But when I put them together, my brain couldn't cope. They made no sense. And to be absolutely one hundred per cent truthful, I wasn't *totally* sure what a penthouse was. I tried to work it all out. I couldn't.

After another moment or two, I said, 'Do my mum and my nan and my brothers live in this penthouse apartment with me?'

'Yes but no,' said Yuri. And to clear up any confusion, he shook his head.

'Oh,' I said. And took a few more quick deep breaths.

The limo drove on. I continued chewing my thumbnail and tried to think. But it was just too hard. That one single impossible thought had suddenly been joined by a thousand more impossible thoughts. And none of them would keep still. They were all rolling round and

round inside my brain. In fact, my entire brain was rolling round inside my head. It was trembling and tumbling and seething and shuddering and heaving and shimmering and splashing and crashing as if it had all the energy of a crazy hyperpotamus.

Eventually, I took my thumbnail away from my mouth and said, 'And they're cool with that? My mum and my nan are actually cool with that and they let me live by myself in a penthouse apartment?'

Yuri shrugged. 'Yes but it's your decision.'

Amazed, I said, '*Is it?*'

'Yes, of course,' said Yuri. 'You went to court and divorced your family in messy public media storm – so it does not matter what they think.'

I stopped breathing again.

I div—

I div—

I divorced . . .

Even more amazed, I said, 'Did I?'

'Yes, of course,' said Yuri. 'Do you not remember this?'

I stared at him. And then – even though I wasn't in any kind of laughing mood – I started to laugh. It was

just a little chuckle at first and then it grew and grew and grew until I was laughing so hard that I could hardly sit up straight. I don't even know why I was laughing. I suppose I just didn't know what else to do.

Yuri Maximovich Krolik frowned at me.

For some reason, this made me laugh even more. But, eventually, I got it together and managed to say, 'I divorced my mum?'

'Yes,' said Yuri.

I hiccupped out a shocked chuckle. 'And my nan?'

'Yes,' said Yuri.

I giggled and then immediately bit my lip. 'And my brothers?'

'Yes,' said Yuri.

'Gosh,' I said. And then I stopped giggling and felt uncomfortable. Harrison is only fourteen months old.

The limo purred on through the darkness. For a couple of minutes, I sat in silence and fiddled about with my hair. It was long and loose and somebody had styled it into fancy twirls. It was nice, but sometimes all you want is a fat unfussy ponytail in a scrunchy. I unravelled a few of the fancy twirls and then I said, 'When?'

Yuri looked at me. 'Yes. When what?'

'When did I divorce my family? When did this happen?'

Yuri poured himself a cup of tea, gave me a very firm look and said, 'Yes but I think you might do something better with your time than waste it by asking riddles that have no answers.'

I stared at him. Confused. Freak is a pretty harsh word in any circumstances, but I can understand why people think Yuri is random.

'You read too many books,' I said. 'You're starting to sound like one.'

'Thank you,' said Yuri. And he smiled.

The limo came to a stop. Yuri jumped up from his seat and opened the passenger door. 'Yes,' he said. 'We are arriving at penthouse apartment. Your housekeeper is waiting for you. Have good sleep. But, remember, tomorrow is early start.'

'Is it?' I felt my stomach sink. I'm not good at early starts. I'm not what you'd call an early bird.

Yuri said, 'Yes. Limousine will pick you up at 5 a.m. so you can go to gym, meet with stylist, sort out eyebrows,

have photo shoot, do interviews, talk to lawyers and still have plenty of time to prepare for appearance at big music festival tomorrow evening.'

'Hey, my eyebrows don't need sorting out,' I snapped. And then I said, 'Music festival? Whoop! I love music festivals. Is it Glastonbury?'

Yuri said, 'I explain tomorrow,' and he held the car door open for me.

I looked around at the others. 'Bye,' I said. But nobody answered. My so-called boyfriend was still listening to his iPod with his eyes closed and my elderly entourage was still asleep. I clambered out of the car. As I brushed past Yuri, I caught a waft of that nice BCK aftershave he was wearing. 'Bye, Yuri,' I said.

Yuri smiled again. 'Yes. Goodbye.'

I started to walk over to my apartment block and then stopped dead in my tracks. Apparently, I lived in a big tall swanky high-rise. Looking up at it, I whispered, 'Where in the world am I?'

This couldn't be my town, could it?

My town has a lot of small, low, ordinary houses in it. And it has a lot of containers. But, as far as I'm aware, it

doesn't have many big, tall, swanky high-rises. I'm not even sure that it has any.

I scratched a Himalaya. *Perhaps we've driven all the way to Ipswich*, I thought. But then another idea struck me. I hesitated, turned and said, 'Yuri?'

'Yes?'

'Did I divorce my dad as well?'

Yuri looked surprised. Shrugging, he said, 'I don't know. I don't think so. This is first time I ever hear you speak of him.'

I looked at the ground.

For ages.

Then I looked up again and nodded. 'I guess that means I didn't. I guess that means I didn't even need to.' And, suddenly feeling very sad, I walked slowly over to where my housekeeper was waiting for me.

Ronni Runnacles @ronneee_r

Curiouser and curiouser.

I was in a strange place looking down on another strange place and my entire brain was buzzing. So was my body. In fact, I was buzzing so much that I felt like I'd swapped lives with a giant bumble bee.

The helicopter tipped sideways and gave me a bee's-eye view of the festival site. Below us – spread out in miniature – was a world made up almost entirely of tents. At the centre of everything was a massive open stage and dotted around it were five enormous white marquees. Each of these marquees stood in its own vast field of mud. Connecting the fields were row upon row of market stalls and gazebos. These were sometimes stripy and sometimes chequered and always every colour you could imagine. In among the stalls and gazebos, random objects like Ferris wheels and bungee-jump towers and giant inflatable hot dogs had crash-landed as if they were alien spacecraft. Further away and stretching right along the banks of the estuary, I could just about make out the dark blobs of hundreds and hundreds more tents. Tiny ones. I can't say for certain what colours they were, but I'm guessing that navy and khaki and camouflage patterns were involved. And milling around everything –

like legions of minuscule black ants – were thousands and thousands and **thousands** of people.

'Whoop,' I shouted into my mouthpiece. I meant it.

Yuri's voice crackled through my headphones. He sounded weird. Like he was talking to me from outer space even though he was actually sitting right next to me.

Yes but you see now? This is much better festival than Glastonbury. This is best music festival in the world. This is Dock 'n' Roll! And you are booked as Number One headlining act. This is your homecoming gig.

'Whoop,' I shouted again. I still meant it.

The helicopter swooped to the right and for a moment all I could see was a thick layer of cloud. I smiled and waved at it. I don't know why. I think it was just because it was the only thing that looked familiar. The helicopter righted itself and hung hovering in mid-air. I pressed my forehead against the glass and looked down. Way below us was a landing pad.

Another voice crackled through my headphones. It was Stuart's.

Spaceman wanted us to roll up in a limo – like all the other losers. You can thank me for this, Ronni. I insisted on the chopper. OK, so we had to drive a few miles out of our way and now we're running a bit late – but why arrive in a limousine if you can arrive in a Sikorsky H-34 Choctaw helicopter?

I turned and saw that Stuart was sitting directly behind me. Even with big orange headphones on and his face half hidden by a microphone, he was still easily the best-looking person in the vicinity. I waved at him and he waved back.

My headphones crackled again. Yuri said,

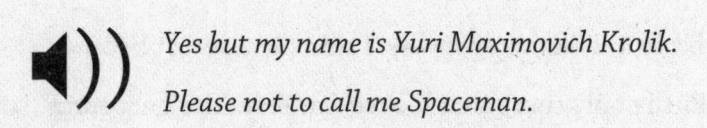

Yes but my name is Yuri Maximovich Krolik. Please not to call me Spaceman.

There was a load more crackling and the sound of static. I can't be sure but – in the middle of all of this – I'm pretty

sure I heard Yuri mutter the word *idiot*.

I turned back round and gazed again over the Dock 'n' Roll site.

Dock 'n' Roll?

It was hard to get my head round.

My home town is famous for having ships and cranes and containers. I don't remember it ever being famous for having the world's best music festival.

Could this really be the same place?

The clouds were the same. The sea was the same. But everything else was different. I couldn't see a single crane or a single ship or a single office block anywhere. I searched the skyline. In the distance and through the mist, I could just about see the derelict gun towers of an ancient fort.

Hmm, I thought. *I suppose it must be then.*

But I still wasn't sure. There was something missing. And I'm not talking about cranes or ships or big grey office blocks. I'm talking about one other small detail. Even though it was small, it was a detail so vitally

important that I knew my town would be lost without it.

I just couldn't quite remember what that detail was.

A third voice crackled in my headphones.

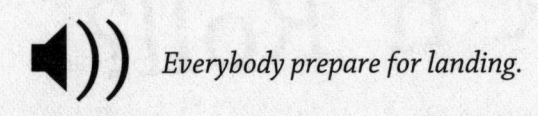 *Everybody prepare for landing.*

Glancing over to the pilot's seat, I saw Dave the Perfect Bodyguard sitting behind the controls. So he could fly helicopters too? Evidently there was a lot more to this man than met the eye.

The helicopter hovered in the air, wobbled from side to side and then began to descend very slowly in a vertical line. For a moment – even with my ears covered – I could hear nothing except the buzzing drone of the engine.

And then we were back on firm ground and the buzzing stopped.

Immediately, a golf buggy came hurtling towards us with a little man inside. It skidded to a stop right next to the helicopter and the little man hopped out in one very quick and jerky movement.

Like the clouds, he looked familiar. But, unlike the

clouds, I didn't have any great urge to wave at him.

Yuri sighed noisily through my headphones. Then he took off his helicopter headgear and said, 'Yes but this is Festival Event Manager. I am thinking he is not a happy man.'

I was thinking that too. The familiar little man looked seriously narked off.

The doors of the helicopter lifted up like the wings of a ladybird. The Festival Event Manager stuck his face into the cabin and said, 'Well, well, well . . . Ronni Runaway! Good of you to finally turn up.'

I took my own headgear off and muttered, 'Gosh. Call that a welcome?' And then, louder, I said, 'We're not that late.'

The Festival Event Manager folded his arms. 'Do you know who Admiral Nelson is?'

Still strapped into my seat in the helicopter, I sat and stared at him. Somewhere inside my head, cogs started turning. And then I whispered, 'Oh my God.'

The FEM stopped looking narked off and started looking smug. 'Admiral Nelson happens to be the gentleman who stands on the column in Trafalgar

Square.' He paused and then added, 'That's in *London*.'

'I do *know* that,' I said.

'Yes,' said Yuri nodding. 'Ronni has sung to sell-out audiences at venues all over world.'

The FEM ignored us both and carried straight on. 'Well, Nelson once made the remark, *Time is everything; five minutes makes the difference between victory and defeat.*'

I shook my head. This was too weird. Eventually – after a lot of head shaking – I just whispered, 'Oh my God,' again.

The FEM flashed me a quick cold smile. 'But I suppose arriving late is the prerogative of a superstar. Beyoncé . . . Gaga . . . Dame Shirley Bassey . . . you're all terrible timekeepers. Never mind. That's why I have the transporter. If you'd care to get in, I'll take you all over to the BCK stage. Hurry along, please. You've left us rather short on time.'

I looked at Yuri and whispered, 'Is this seriously who I think it is?'

Before Yuri could reply, Stuart Bolan leaned forward and muttered, 'Dunno. But whoever he is – he thinks he's the

King of the Cockroaches.' And then he grinned and added, 'Actually, you can scrub the roach part. He's just a—'

Yuri said, 'Yes but Festival Event Manager is correct. Hurry up, please. We have urgent appointment at BCK stage.'

Stuart and I sniggered, undid our seat belts and clambered out. In spite of the shabby welcome, I was feeling good. In actual fact, I was feeling better than good. Because the simple truth was that I'd just arrived by helicopter to headline the best music festival in the world and now I was sniggering over a private joke with my boyfriend, Stuart Bolan.

Otherwise known as

StuBo.

Otherwise known as the boy *everybody* fancies.

The word *good* didn't even come close to covering it.

The King of the Cockroaches drove us across the bumpy landing strip, turned left at a field filled with enormous silver motor homes, continued past some huge black tour buses, took a sharp right by some colossal

white wigwams and eventually came to a standstill behind the central open-air stage I'd seen from the helicopter.

Up close and able to appreciate its proper proportions, it was truly enormous.

It was even more enormous than the stage at the Copper Bowl.

In fact, this stage was – without any doubt – the Top Trump of all the Super Stages.

SUPER STAGES

THE BCK STAGE AT DOCK'n' ROLL

STAGE SIZE : EPIC
RIGGING : LOADS
THIS TRUMP CARD BEATS ALL OTHER CARDS !

I jumped out of the golf buggy and looked around in a daze. People were rushing about in a field of mud and shouting into headsets. They were wearing T-shirts with

my face on. Among them, security guards were walking around in wellies and mumbling into walkie-talkies. On a raft of muddy gym mats, a group of dancers in black leotards was standing together in a huddle and looking anxious. One of them – the tallest and coolest – spotted me and said, 'There she is!'

Another dancer said, 'Come on, Ronni. We need to go!' And she pointed upward.

I looked up. The enormous stage frowned down on me. On each corner, there was a round yellow tower topped by a pointed turret. The entire construction looked less like a stage and more like an ancient castle. Only yellower. Yuri appeared next to me. 'Yes. It is BCK stage. The biggest outdoor stage in world. Named after billionaire local designer.'

'Whoop,' I said. But it sort of got stuck in my throat.

'Yes,' said Yuri. 'Whoop!'

From his seat in the golf buggy, the FEM flashed us both another one of his quick cold smiles and said, '*Whoop?* How wise.' And then he turned the ignition key and skittered away over the bumpy ground.

We all stood together and watched him go. For a

moment, none of us spoke. But then Yuri coughed and said, 'Yes. This man is douchebag.'

Stuart laughed, clapped Yuri on the back and said, 'Nice one, mate.'

Yuri responded with a nod and a stiff little smile. I smiled too. I think it's the friendliest conversation I've ever heard them have.

Yuri said, 'Yes. And now you have to be on stage.'

'But I can't go now,' I said. 'I'm not r

But nobody heard me. High above us, a band had begun to play. They were so loud that I could feel every single beat thump through my body. It was like someone had changed my personal setting to vibrate.

Yuri took hold of my arm and led me over to a metal disc on the ground. Cupping his hand to my ear, he shouted, '**Stand here. No time for discussion. We are very late.**'

I grabbed hold of his arm. There was a lump rising in my throat. This was the stuff of dreams.

Me.

Headlining.

At a festival.

In front of

thousands

and

thousands

of

adoring

fans.

But there's a very big difference between dreaming and actually *doing*. And suddenly I wasn't sure how much of a *doe*r I actually was.

I swallowed down the throat lump and said, 'I can't.'

Yuri looked confused. He pointed up at the stage, then pointed to his ear and shouted, 'Yes but I cannot hear you.'

I bit my lip and tried to think, but it was too hard because my head had filled up with fog. Was I really Ronni Runaway? Everyone seemed to think so. But . . .

Yuri said, 'Yes. Lift will take you slowly up to stage.' And then he gave a rare grin and added, 'Scream if you want to go faster!'

I stared at him.

Scream

if

you

want

to

go

faster.

Yuri's words flew around in my head. And, as they swooped and spun, the fog thinned out and then vanished. And suddenly I could see everything very clearly.

The queue in the dining hall.

Seaside Sibyl in her
fortune-telling booth.

The dodgem track.

The head-on collision.

I could see everything that had brought me to this point. It was playing in my head like a slide show. And

nothing about any of it suggested I'd actually be any good up there on that stage.

Panicking, I put my lips right up to Yuri's ear and said, 'I've never done this before. I don't even know if I can sing. I don't know how this has happened. I think I've got concussion or something.'

Yuri turned to look at me. He was looking even more confused than before. But, suddenly, his face brightened and he said, 'Yes. It is just nerves.'

'IT IS *NOT* NERVES,' I said. Actually, I think I screamed it.

Yuri pointed at the stage, then pointed to his ear and gave me an apologetic shrug.

With enormous self-control, I bit back the urge to chuck a wobbly and glanced around desperately to see if there was anyone nearby who could help me out. And then my heart sank like a shopping trolley. Clearly Stuart Bolan wasn't going to help. Because, in the few minutes that my back had been turned, my so-called boyfriend had wandered over to the huddle of dancers and was now engaged in a blatant and unashamed act of public snoggery.

'Whoop,' I said flatly. And then I realized that I didn't

actually care very much and just muttered, 'Idiot!'

I glanced around again. And this time my spirits soared. A woman was rushing towards me. She was wearing a headset and a T-shirt with my face on it – but none of that fooled me. I knew her. And she knew me. And I knew she knew I was not the kind of person who could ever stand on that stage and make a proper genuine effort.

'Mrs Booley,' I shouted in relief. I was so pleased to see her I practically hugged her.

But Mrs Booley didn't look quite so pleased to see me. 'It's Mrs Clooney,' she shouted back. 'I remarried.' She tucked the edge of her grey bob behind one ear, looked at Yuri and shouted, 'Is she ready to go, Mr Krolik?'

'Hey, excuse me,' I said. 'Talk to the organ-grinder – not the monkey!'

Yuri said, 'Yes but she is.' And then he did something I've never seen him do before. He winked.

'OK. Time to get moving,' shouted Mrs Clooney into her headset.

'But—' I said.

'No buts,' said Mrs C.

To my horror, the metal disc I was standing on began to rise up and up – away from the mud and the dancers and the snoggery and the people with their headsets and handsets and loudhailers.

'I'm not ready,' I shouted down.

Mrs C tilted back her head, smiled at me patiently and shouted back, 'You'll be fine. This isn't difficult. Not for a clever girl like you.'

'But I'm just stupid boring Veronica Runnacles,' I said hopelessly. I didn't even bother to shout. I knew nobody was listening.

But somehow Yuri Maximovich Krolik must have heard me. Because he cupped his hands together and shouted, 'Yes but you cannot seriously think this. You are not stupid boring person. You have never been.'

And then he was gone. And Mrs Clooney and Stuart Bolan and Dave the Perfect Bodyguard were gone too. And as for my so-called entourage, they're not even worth a mention. I hadn't seen either of them all day.

It was just me now.

On my own.

In a spotlight.

On the biggest stage in the entire world.

'Whoop,' I whispered.

The intro music soared to a crescendo and then abruptly stopped. The spotlight around me grew hotter and brighter. In front of me – through the evening gloom – I could see a great big sea of waving arms and floating flags and flashing camera lenses.

It was like a dream come true.

Only I **really** wanted to wake up.

'I'm not ready,' I whispered. 'I haven't had time to focus.'

And suddenly a strange noise filled the air. For a moment, I couldn't work out what it was. It sounded a bit like a **gigantic** road drill. Or a billion monkeys chattering in the exact same tree. Or a million car engines trying to start, and failing.

Hee hee hee hee. hee

And then I realized what it was.

It was the sound of one hundred and thirty-five thousand individual people laughing.

At me.

'Gosh,' I whispered. And then, louder, I said, 'Just shut up, will you?'

For a fraction of a second, the laughter stopped. And then it came back.

Hee hee hee hee.

A movement out of the corner of my right eye made me turn my head. My backing dancers were arriving on the stage and striking their opening poses. Even in the glare of the spotlight, I could see they were edgy and nervous and throwing me quick glances of pure panic. The coolest and tallest of them had abandoned her stage position and was hurrying towards me. 'Ronni,' she hissed as soon as she reached me, 'what the heck are you waiting for? Just start singing the stupid flipping song!'

Clamping my fist around the microphone I suddenly realized was in front of me, I hissed back, 'I can't. I'm not ready. I need at least another five minutes.'

The dancer pulled a face. 'Just sort it out, Ronni. You're making us all look bad.'

'Thanks a bunch,' I snapped. And then I made a

weird hiccupping noise. There was a lump stuck in my throat and it was so big that it's a medical miracle I didn't choke on it. I stopped clamping hold of the mike and clamped hold of my mouth instead.

In front of me, the huge crowd began to slowly clap their hands.

Clap. Clap. Clap. Clap.

The lump in my throat began to rise. Dropping my hands, I took a deep gasp of evening air and muttered, 'I think I'm going to be sick.'

My magnified mutter rumbled like thunder across the field. There was more laughter from the crowd and more slow hand clapping.

Clap. Clap. Clap. Clap.

'Oh God,' I groaned.

Another movement caught my attention. This time, from the left. I turned. On the far side of the enormous stage and hidden from the hostile eyes of the crowd, I

could just about see a dark figure. To my complete and utter astonishment, this dark figure was facing my way with welcoming outstretched arms.

Frozen inside the single spotlight, I stood and frowned into the darkness. As my eyes adjusted, the figure of a teenage boy began to take shape.

A BOY

WHO WAS
QUITE TALL AND
QUITE THIN AND
QUITE QUIET AND

QUITE ORDINARY-LOOKING . . .

. . . and quite simply the kindest and most caring and most dependable boy I've ever met.

If I'd had a car horn handy, I'd have honked it.

'Give me a second,' I said to one hundred and thirty-five thousand slowly clapping people. And then I fled gratefully to the wings into the waiting rescuing arms of Yuri Maximovich Krolik.

A split second before I reached Yuri, I noticed the long line of cable he was holding. And I noticed him drop the cable on the stage and give a thumbs-up to one of the stage crew. And then he gave his aching arms a big shake. I seriously noticed all of this in one split second. It was like time had slowed right down . . .

And then it sped right up again and I crashed straight into him.

Thwack!

Yuri's arms flew back open. And then they folded awkwardly round me as he tried to stop us both from falling over in a heap. I've never been hugged by a boy before. If this experience is anything to go by, it feels a lot like being hugged by a surfboard.

My face burst into flames. I wriggled out of Yuri's accidental hug, stepped back and said, 'Ouch.' And then I muttered, 'I'm sorry. I thought . . .' And then I shut up.

Yuri looked shocked. He said, 'Yes but . . .' And then he shut up too.

Meanwhile, the crowd were still going

Clap. Clap. Clap. Clap.

'Oh my God,' I wailed. 'This has got to be the *worst* dream ever!'

Yuri frowned and pushed a strand of his mousy hair away from his grey eyes. My face burned a little hotter. Up this close, it was impossible not to notice that Yuri has surprisingly nice eyes. I could see the sky and the sea and the whole world in them. Until that moment, I never knew a pair of grey eyes could show me so much. But

that's because I'd never really looked into any.

Yuri's nice eyes looked straight into mine and he said, 'It's time for you to wake up.'

I stared at him.

Had he just said wake up?

Hope swelled up inside me. He *knew*. He knew this wasn't real. Crossing my fingers, I said, 'What's going on, Yuri? Tell me what's happening?'

But Yuri just shrugged. And then he frowned and said, 'Dreaming is all very good, but it's what we do when we wake up that counts.'

It was my turn to frown. This is the kind of comment I expect from Seaside Sibyl or my nan. I don't expect it from anyone I go to school with.

'But I don't even know if I *am* dreaming,' I said. 'So how can I wake up? I don't even know who the heck I am at the moment! I'm seriously flipping confused!'

I think I was starting to get a bit hysterical.

Yuri's forehead crumpled into the mother of all frowns. 'You are you,' he said. 'Ronni Runnacle. And I like you very much. But you need to stop living in your dreams and start changing your reality.' And then he

leaned forward and kissed me – very gently – on my own frowning forehead.

My mouth opened, but no words came out. I was utterly speechless. The truth is that I'd never been kissed by a boy before. Not even by Stuart Bolan and he was supposed to be my boyfriend, wasn't he? Not that he actually mattered. Because being kissed on the forehead by Yuri Maximovich Krolik felt just like being touched by a single second of intense wonderland sunshine.

Eventually, I said, 'You know who I am? And you like me anyway? Even though I'm nobody special?'

Yuri shrugged again and, this time, his shrug came with a little smile. Holding out his hands to me, he said, 'Ronni, wake up! Come on, wake up!'

And that's the great thing about a good story. You can never know for sure what's going to happen next. Because, just a few seconds before, I'd been desperate to wake up and escape from all this, and now that I had the chance, I suddenly didn't want to. Because this dream – if it *was* a dream – had just transformed into . . .

THE BEST
DREAM
EVER!

So I squeezed Yuri's hand and said, 'Whoop!' And then
I let it go and said, 'There's no way this ends here. It's
just starting to get really interesting. This is brilliant.
I need to find out what happens next.' I was already
walking back to the spotlight.

Yuri said, 'Yes but—'

'It's OK.' I called. 'I'm having the best dream

ever. Nothing can go wrong. There's nothing I can't do!'

And I believed it. And I was still believing it as I stood blinking in the glare of the spotlight and glared at the laughing clapping crowd.

Slowly the crowd stopped clapping.

I lifted my chin up and shouted, 'You finished?'

There was another burst of road drilling and monkey chatter. A few more slow hand claps. A few more jeers.

I sucked in my cheeks and rolled my eyes. Then I looked around at my backing dancers and shouted fiercely, 'You ready?' I suddenly had a whole extra heap of attitude. In fact, I probably had more attitude than Ming the Merciless. Whoever she is.

My dancers nodded fiercely back.

Someone near the front of the crowd shouted, 'Are you still feeling sick?' There was another explosion of laughter.

I took hold of the microphone and said,

'Damn right I'm feeling sick . . . plain sick! So stop snickering before I pull out of here with a sick note. And quit the slow hand clapping too because it gets my goat and it sickens my chickens. So have some respect y'all . . . Cos I'm sicker than the average sick girl and more random than a bag of sick 'n' mix. I've got a black belt in sick-boxing, I'm a star of *Sickly Come Dancing* and I've got more words than the sictionary. So let me hear you make some *positive* noise for the one and only Lady Sick Sick!'

I think even Ming the Merciless would have been scared.

But the effect on the crowd was magic. They erupted. My backing band seized the advantage and quickly launched into my hit single *Docksy Lady* and I opened my mouth and started to sing. And, to my utter delight, the sound that came out of my mouth was really, really good. Yuri was right. I was special. I turned and waved at him but he didn't wave back. I didn't care. I was wearing those amazing gold boots and the matching jacket and shorts so short my nan would have gagged on her gobstoppers. I was feeling totally and utterly delicious.

And all I wanted was for this dream to go on and on forever. Because this was exactly how it was supposed to be. My backing dancers had binned their bad attitudes and were back to loving me. And in the VIP enclosure, I could see Beyoncé and Jay-Z and that man from Coldplay and they were loving me even more. And far, far into the fading light, I could see my one hundred and thirty-five thousand fans waving and clapping and going totally berserk at my every single move. And some of them were holding up flags and banners that had my name on and one other lone fan was holding up a

big flag that just said . . .

Sadie Slow Groove.

I stopped singing. Behind me, my band continued to play.
I spun round to face them and waved my arms until *they*
came to a stop too. All over the stage, my backing dancers
shook their stuff through a few more moves before
slowing to an awkward standstill. It was like watching
their batteries run out. The tallest and coolest of them
looked at me and shouted, 'What the *heck* is the
matter now?'

Pointing at the flag, I said, 'I'm not having that. No
way! Whoever is holding that flag can just jog off right
now.'

There was a rumble of mumbling from the crowd.
Somebody shouted, 'What's your problem?' I can't
be sure but I think it might have been that man from
Coldplay.

I put my hands on my hips. And then – to one hundred and thirty-five thousand people – I said, 'I'll tell you what my problem is. That girl ruins everything.'

There was total silence. *Good*, I thought. *That's told them.*

And then a new noise filled the night air. It wasn't applause and it wasn't shouts or jeers or road drills or monkey chatter or slow hand claps. It was this:

Boo Boo Boo Boo Boo Boo Boo Boo Boo Boo Boo Boo Boo Boo Boo Boo Boo Boo Boo

And without a doubt, it was truly the most terrible sound I'd ever heard. And it got louder and

louder

and

louder

and louder

until I couldn't stand another second of it. And then I dropped my microphone and fled to the side of the stage and the comforting arms of Yuri. But when I got there I found that Yuri had gone.

Ronni Runnacles @ronneee_r

Sometimes it's impossible to avoid the truth – even when you're dreaming. #imgettingreallydeepnow

It doesn't matter whether you're wide awake in the real world or lost in a daze in Wonderland, the following sentence will always be true: it's not nice to be booed off a stage by one hundred and thirty-five thousand people.

It's not nice at all. In fact, it sucks.

If this has ever happened to you, you'll know exactly what I'm talking about. And you'll also know that – whatever positive spin you try to put on it – you always end up face to face with the same upsetting realization: Either

> a) one hundred and thirty-five thousand people have collectively made a massive mistake
>
> *or*
>
> b) you have.

I sort of knew it was (b).

The next day, I sat alone on the floor of my penthouse apartment and tried to figure out precisely what my serious mistake was. It wasn't easy. The more I mulled it over, the more mistakes I spotted.

1. I'd arrived late. And time is everything. Five minutes can make the difference between victory and defeat.

2. I wasn't focused enough. George Clooney did not conquer Hollywood without being properly focused.

3. I should not have let myself get distracted by Yuri Maximovich Krolik and his nice grey eyes.

4. I should have worn something more practical than gold boots and a gold jacket and a pair of stupidly short shorts. No way is that an outfit that screams the words sick and fierce.

5. I shouldn't have let a random fan of Sadie Slow Groove wind me up.

My mind drifted back to mistake number three. *What was all that about?* I sighed and moodily flicked a blob of tomato ketchup at my white minimalist wall. I don't know why. I think I did it just because I could.

'I can do whatever the heck I want,' I said out loud to my empty room. And then I frowned because I wasn't one hundred per cent sure who *I* actually was.

Everything in my head felt so mashed-up and confused. For a while, at the festival, it had cleared. Or I'd thought it had. But now the weird foggy feeling was back. It was the same kind of feeling I have when I watch telly on the internet and everyone's lips are slightly out of time with the sound. It was putting me in a bad mood. I squeezed a dollop of red sauce on to a spoon and lobbed another ketchup paint bomb at the wall.

'Focus, Ronni,' I said out loud. 'Who *are* you?'

I focused.

I was Miss Ronni Runaway, Queen of urban beats, hip-hop and rap, Superstar of UK garage and First Lady of British soul funk. *I* had enjoyed seven hit singles, a

Number One album in fifty-nine different countries, an award-winning Bond theme and a very high-profile legal battle with Piers Morgan.

I was the stuff of dreams.

'Big flipping whoop,' I said, and catapulted more ketchup.

The ketchup dripped down the wall and made the shape of a face.

'Weirder and weirder,' I muttered.

I shut my eyes tight and shook my head to clear it. And then I opened my eyes again. But the saucy face was still staring back at me. Admittedly, you needed to put your head on one side and go slightly boss-eyed to see it, but it was **definitely** a face. Dumping the spoon and the ketchup bottle on the polished wooden floor, I crept

closer to the wall. Then I put my head on the other side and looked at the blob art again. And this time I could clearly see that I was looking at the face of a little boy.

And it was a little boy I recognised.

For a second, I was so shocked I couldn't move. And then I smiled and said, 'Joe?'

Joe is my third brother. He won't eat anything unless it comes with a side helping of ketchup. And that includes custard. My smile grew. I reached back, grabbed my unusual art equipment and lobbed him his side order.

Joe's face disappeared. The tomato sauce oozed down the wall and morphed into the outline of a giggling big baby.

'Harrison!' My face broke out into a huge grin.
I pulled back my ears and stuck out my tongue. It's impossible not to turn into a great big softhead whenever

you look at Harrison. Even when he's just a piece of weird tomato-ketchup wall art.

'Bet you wish you were here with me,' I said. 'You could chuck as much food about as you liked.'

And then I frowned. When had I last seen him? When had I last seen **any** of my brothers?

My head thickened with interference again. I focused and forced myself to think through it.

Am I really living all alone in this posh penthouse apartment or is my family no further away than another frame of mind?

I was now thinking so much that I was struggling to understand my own thoughts. I chucked the question out of my head and turned to another one:

Who the heck am I?

And, despite all the fog and snow and loose wires and bad connections, I found an answer.

I was Miss Ronni Runaway. My headlining appearance at the Dock 'n' Roll festival had been a total flop, my so-called boyfriend had dumped me for a backing dancer and my entourage had completely disappeared. Even my bodyguard and my housekeeper didn't seem that fussed about me.

In fact, the only person who did seem to like me was Yuri Maximovich Krolik.

He'd phoned a few hours earlier. There was no mention of The Kiss. Instead, he said, 'Yes. I have plan. I have very good plan. This evening, you will be guest on prime-time popular chatting show. You can discuss all messy business and apologize for angry bad things you said about Sadie Slow Groove. And general publics will understand you and like you again.'

'No way,' I said immediately. 'There is **no way** I'm

going on telly and apologizing to Sadie Slowgrove! I just can't do it.'

'Yes but it is Slow *Groove*,' corrected Yuri. 'And you can do it. It's easy. S. O. R. R. Y. You begin at the beginning and go on till you come to the end and then stop.'

'Oh whatever,' I snapped. 'I'm not flipping well going to.'

I heard Yuri sigh. 'Yes but you do not help yourself. It is much better if you discuss messy business. You should trust me on this.'

And, straight away, I said, 'I don't trust anyone, Yuri.'

There was a long silence on the end of the line. Eventually, Yuri said, 'Yes but you must trust and believe in people or life becomes impossible.'

Yuri Maximovich Krolik might be a bit random, but he's also incredibly deep.

I sniffed and stared at my boring minimalist white walls. 'You read too many books,' I said. 'You're seriously starting to sound like one.'

And even though I couldn't see his face, I could tell that Yuri was chuffed. His voice suddenly had a smile in it. He said, 'Yes but this is quotation from Anton

Chekhov. He was very intense Russian writer who wrote very intense Russian literatures. He understood life well because – in only forty-four short years – he lived a lot of it. And now you must try to live it and understand it too. Limousine will pick you up at 3 p.m. for taking you to TV studio. I will be inside.' And with that he put the phone down.

And now it was exactly 3 p.m. Outside, several storeys down at street level, I could hear a car horn honking. A memory of something or someone flashed across my mind, but before I had a chance to properly make sense of it, it was gone again. A loud knock on my living-room door interrupted my thoughts.

'Come in,' I shouted.

My housekeeper stuck her head round the door. And then she saw the sauce art on my walls and said, 'And who do you think is going to clean that up?'

My face went hot. 'They're my walls.'

My housekeeper scowled. 'They might be. But I'm not a skivvy. And if you treat me like one I'll hand my notice in and you can find some other fool to wipe the food off your walls.'

'OK,' I said. 'I'm sorry.' And then I muttered, 'Gosh!'

My housekeeper scowled at me again and said, 'You're sorry? *I'm* sorry! I had a nice little job cutting hair in a salon in Ipswich before I took this position. Worst mistake I ever made. And to think *I* was the woman who once blow-dried Madonna's hair! How the mighty fall, eh?'

A bell rang in my brain somewhere. But then it stopped ringing. I shrugged and said, 'Did you *actually* want something or have you just come in here to moan at me?'

My housekeeper said, 'Mr Krolik is waiting outside with the car.'

'Big whoop,' I said, and jumped to my feet. 'I can't breathe in this situation.' And, grabbing my coat, I rushed past her and stormed down the stairs to join Yuri.

Ronni Runnacles @ronneee_r

Guess who's trending?

'*Showbiz* Sibyl? Are you serious?' I searched Yuri's face for a sign that he was joking. I didn't find one.

'Yes,' said Yuri. 'Showbiz Sibyl. Everyone is talking about her. She is world-famous celebrity and very popular with general publics. Her show – *Teatime with Sibyl* – is biggest programme on British and American television networks. We are very lucky to be given solo guest spot with such short notices. Very lucky.'

Even with a brain that felt like it was full of broken biscuits, I was suspicious. There are some people you just don't forget. No matter what weird stuff happens. They float around in your head like driftwood. *Showbiz Sibyl*? It couldn't be . . . Could it?

There was a buzzing sound and a bulb on the wall changed from red to green. A woman wearing a headset said, 'OK, Miss Runaway, you're on in ten seconds.' And then she linked her arm through mine and marched me over to a door marked STUDIO ONE.

'I'm not sure about this,' I said. To be honest, I wasn't sure about anything any more.

Yuri followed behind us. 'You'll be fine,' he said. 'It's easy. All you have to do is begin at the beginning and go

on till you come to the end and then stop.'

The woman with the headset said, 'You're on now,' and pushed me through the door.

I stumbled through it and into the blinding light of Studio One. In front of me, a seated audience started to clap. Behind me, in a very loud whisper, I heard Yuri say, 'And make sure you answer the questions honestly. It is very important!'

I walked forward into the light.

Showbiz Sibyl? It couldn't possibly be . . . Could it?

On an armchair in front of the audience sat an old woman. She was wearing a sparkly silver headscarf, a purple shawl and a silky leopard-print blouse.

'Oh my God,' I whispered. *Because it absolutely totally could!*

Showbiz Sibyl stood up, held out her arms and beamed at me with a massive gold-toothed smile. 'Hello, Ronni, my little peanut. Long time no see.' And then she stopped smiling, raised one terrifying eyebrow and added, 'Shouldn't you be in after-school club or something?'

The audience laughed.

I said, 'Er . . . I dunno. I . . .'

Showbiz Sibyl raised her hand to silence me. 'I'm only teasing, kiddo.' Then she winked and added, 'And, even if you were, you can rely on me to keep *shtum*. This little chat won't go any further than you, me and my twenty million viewers.'

The audience laughed again.

I gulped.

Showbiz Sibyl patted the backrest of a second armchair and said, 'Come over here and join me, sweetheart.'

I did as I was told. There was something about Showbiz Sibyl that forced me to.

Showbiz Sibyl greeted me with a hug and kissed the air near both of my cheeks. Up close, she smelt just like a tub of old 2ps. She seriously needed some of that BCK stuff.

We sat down. It didn't make me feel any more relaxed though. *Had she really said twenty million viewers?*

'Now look here, kiddo,' said Showbiz Sibyl, 'as much as I'm tickled pink to see you, I'm not sure how fans of Sadie Slow Groove will be feeling if they're watching the telly right now. You upset a lot of people at the Dock 'n' Roll Festival. A lot of people. And your remarks at the Brit Awards ruffled a fair few feathers too. The

newspapers haven't got a good word to say about you these days and even the prime minister has remarked on your behaviour. In the House of Commons yesterday he declared that you were a bad influence on the young people of Great Britain. But I'm not one to judge, Ronni. Oh no. Not me. I prefer to get to the heart of the matter. To understand. And, as I understand it, something is troubling you very deeply, my dear. So I think it's about time we had a serious chat to find out what that something is.'

There was a spontaneous burst of approval from the studio audience. A few people cheered. Somebody shouted, 'Sadie Slow Groove rocks!' The audience erupted into more cheers and some laughter.

Showbiz Sibyl held up one hand and they were quiet again. I gulped and fiddled with my hair. Somebody backstage had combed it all straight and fixed a fancy ribbon into it. It was nice but sometimes all you really want is a fat unfussy ponytail in a scrunchy. I didn't feel like me. Instead, I felt like a stupid character from some book I'd been reading – that weird one about the weird girl who follows a random rabbit down a random hole.

What was it called again? *Black Beauty*?

Showbiz Sibyl leaned forward and gazed at me with her intense blue eyes. 'So, Ronni, how would you say that life is treating you at the moment?'

'OK,' I said.

For a moment there was silence. Not a sound came from Sibyl and not a sound came from the audience. All I could hear was my heart thumping. I didn't like it. Switching on my tough face, I lifted up my chin and said, 'Actually it's better than OK. It's amazing.'

Showbiz Sibyl smiled. 'Is that right?'

'Yes,' I said. 'It is.'

Yuri's words of advice spun round in my head.

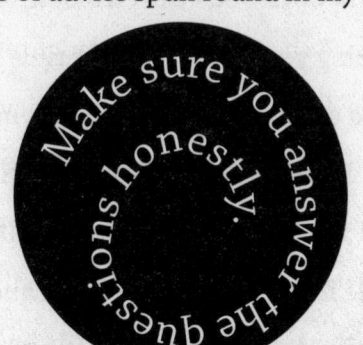

Make sure you answer the questions honestly.

I crossed my fingers and waited for Sibyl to ask me something else, but she didn't. It made me nervous.

'Actually,' I said, filling the silence, 'it's better than

amazing. It's totally zing! I've had three multi-platinum albums, I've dueted with will.i.am, Shakira and Michael Bublé, my latest album won a Nobel Peace Prize, I've recorded the nation's favourite Bond theme and I've got more followers on Twitter than anybody else in the world.' I sat back in my chair and folded my arms. 'That's not bad, is it? Considering I should be at school.'

A few people in the audience clapped. Not many though.

Showbiz Sibyl smiled again. 'Well, Ronni, I hate to burst your bubble but you aren't the most followed person on Twitter. Not any more. Trends change. Over the last couple of days, you've been losing followers like you've been losing your memory. Last time my researcher looked, you had seven. And one of them's me.'

'Oh,' I said. '*Seven?*' And then I smirked it out and said, 'Yeah, but I bet the other six are top-quality followers.' A load of people in the audience laughed and I smirked a bit more. But I wasn't enjoying this programme very much. If I could've, I'd have changed the channel.

Suddenly, I frowned. *How the heck did she know I was having problems with my memory?*

Showbiz Sibyl must have been able to read my mind. Staring straight into my eyes, she said, 'I have hunches, dear. And my hunches are never wrong. It's a gift, you see.'

'Oh,' I said.

'So what's the problem between you and Sadie Slow Groove?'

The silence returned. Everyone in the entire studio seemed to be holding their breath.

I shrugged and tried to keep my smirk glued into position, but it kept sliding off. 'She just winds me up,' I muttered.

Showbiz Sibyl smiled. 'Is that right?'

'Yes,' I said a little louder. 'It is.'

Sibyl's eyes narrowed and she pressed her glossy red lips hard together. Something told me that the next thing she said was going to be very important. I don't know how I knew this – I just did. Maybe I have hunches too. Crossing my fingers, I followed the example of the audience and held my breath.

In a weird dreamy voice, Showbiz Sibyl said, 'Have you ever stopped to consider how Sadie might be feeling? If

not, you should try. A little consideration is something you can **never** give away. It always comes back to you.'

There was a burst of applause from the audience. More bells started ringing in my head. I'd heard those words before, hadn't I? Confused, I said, 'But that sounds just like . . . like . . .'

Showbiz Sibyl smiled. 'Like something your nan would say?'

I stared at her and nodded.

Showbiz Sibyl smiled. Or I think she did. To be honest, she'd suddenly gone so completely fuzzy and blurry that I could hardly even see her any more. Leaning forward, she patted me on the arm and said, 'Now that we've mentioned her, I think I should show you this.'

The studio darkened and everyone in the audience tilted their head upward to look at a huge square of light that had suddenly appeared on a wall behind us. Sibyl and I turned round so we could see it too. As I watched, the face of an oldish woman appeared. She had spiky copper hair and was wearing a very low scooped neckline. She also had big diamond earrings and a matching diamond nose stud. Instantly, the broken biscuits and fog and

clouds and interference and driftwood vanished from my head. 'Nan,' I whispered, 'Is that you?'

And then – for the millionth time – I frowned. *Diamond earrings? A matching diamond nose stud?* It *was* my nan. But she was . . . different.

Showbiz Sibyl said, 'Good evening, Brenda. Thanks for joining us.'

In the huge square of light on the wall of the studio, my nan fiddled with something inside her left ear and muttered, 'This ain't working – I can't hear a sodding dickie bird.'

Showbiz Sibyl turned to the nearest camera and beamed. 'Excuse us. We seem to have a slight technical hitch, but I can assure you that our sound engineers will have everything fixed in the twinkling of an eye. We'll be talking to Ronni's nan – live from her home in Los Angeles – very, very soon.'

'Huh?' I said. And then I followed that up with, 'What the heck is my nan doing in LA? She hardly ever even goes to Ipswich!'

Showbiz Sibyl's eyebrows shot up. 'Crikey! You really *have* lost touch with your folks, haven't you? She's been living over there a little while now.'

'Has she?' I looked up at the wall. My nan was still poking herself in the ear and mumbling. In front of her was a glass of pink champagne and behind her was a palm tree.

Sibyl shrugged. 'By the time she left, she was the richest woman in Britain. So the world was her lobster really, wasn't it?'

My brain nearly fell out of my mouth. 'My *nan* . . . is the *richest* woman in Britain?'

'*Was,*' corrected Showbiz Sibyl. 'She's the richest woman in America now.'

'But . . . But she can't be,' I said.

Sibyl shrugged again. 'She can be, sweetheart, and she is. You aren't the only person in your family who has big ideas. Your nan's online auction site gets more hits these days than eBay, and I suppose the fact that she married a billionaire didn't hurt her bank balance either.'

'My nan has an online auction site?' I said. And then – before Sibyl could answer – I added, '*She married a billionaire?*'

Showbiz Sibyl shook her head in astonishment. 'Of course! Didn't you know about that? The papers are

always full of pictures of her and . . . Oh, hang on, the sound guys are telling me the line is fixed.'

She turned back to face my nan on the wall. 'Hello, Brenda. Can you hear me now?'

Somewhere in front of a palm tree in Los Angeles, my nan smiled and waved. Then she said, 'Hello, Sibyl, I certainly can. And hello, Ronni. I've missed you, lady. We all have.'

My nan was so far away from me that her lips were out of sync with her words. I blinked. My vision was going a bit fuzzy.

My nan said, 'Are you OK?'

'Yeah,' I said. It was the most I could manage.

My nan's eyes narrowed. 'So why aren't you smiling then? You're as pretty as a picture when you smile, Ronni. Once upon a time, you were always smiling. Before all that messy business with your dad.'

And then she muttered something that triggered a loud BLEEP. But I heard it anyway. 'Selfish bloody man!'

'Don't, Nan,' I said in a panic. 'Please. There are twenty million people watching. I don't want to talk about him.'

My nan's shoulders rose and fell and a second later we all heard a loud sighing sound. Then she said, 'Well, you need to talk about him sometime, Ronni. You can't keep on pretending you don't care.'

'Excuse me,' I snapped. '*He's* the one who doesn't care! I might as well not exist. Now he's got his new life, he doesn't want to know me any more. He doesn't want to know any of us.'

My nan did another big time-delayed sigh. 'Your dad has cleared off and not been in touch and you're upset about it. I'm not surprised. We all are. But shutting yourself off from everybody and muddling along with a whole heap of anger locked up in your belly isn't going to make you feel better. It'll just make you bitter.'

'I'm not bitter,' I spat.

My nan looked doubtful. 'But you aren't exactly sweet as candy either. And that's why you're taking it out on this poor Sadie girl. But she hasn't done anything wrong, Ronni. She's been just as knocked for six by this business as you have. It's not her fault. This is a mess made by adults.'

I felt my cheeks go hot. Because – whether I like it or

not – my nan is almost always right.

My nan's lips began to move again. A second later, she said, 'Listen, lady, I know I'm in LA but if ever you want to talk to me, you can. My internet business . . . my billions . . . this twelve-bedroom villa in Beverley Hills . . . paintballing with the Beckhams . . . none of it means diddly squat compared to your happiness. Whenever you want to talk, I'll be there. Like a shot. Ken will understand. Sometimes there's nothing you need more than a natter with your nan when the whole world has gone downside up.'

'Thanks,' I whispered. And then I sat up very suddenly in my seat and said, '*Ken?*'

My nan smiled and said something else, but this time the sound didn't follow. She just kept on chattering away and I couldn't hear her. It was as if somebody had pressed a button and switched her to MUTE. In frustration and despair, I put my hand to my mouth to stop myself from shouting out to her. As I watched, the camera zoomed in on a huge diamond wedding ring on her finger and then it pulled back again so that I could see more of my nan and more of the palm tree and more and more until,

suddenly, I was looking at somebody else too. Somebody with slicked-back rockabilly hair, shaggy L-shaped sideburns and a little round earring in his ear. My nan was smiling and holding hands with Bouncy Castle Ken!

I lowered my hand and whispered, 'Oh my God!'

Showbiz Sibyl said, 'I'm afraid we're going to have to leave the satellite link there. We're having more technical difficulties. But wasn't it lovely to see Ronni's nan looking so happy with her tycoon husband?'

The studio audience roared a collective YES of agreement.

I shook my head in shock. 'She married the bouncy-castle guy!'

The audience laughed.

Showbiz Sibyl said, 'Well, bouncy castles aren't really his line of business these days. He went bust. Something to do with truanting teenagers and a dispute over a wall. But what a stroke of luck that turned out to be! Ken now has his own bestselling ranges of luxury scents and clothing – and he owns the Dock 'n' Roll festival. Your nan did well to bag him. There's a whole line of older

ladies who'd love to have him squeezing their toothpaste.'

'Oh my God,' I said again. But, even so, I smiled. Because it was suddenly hard not to. At the end of that satellite link, my nan had looked really happy. Happier than I'd ever seen her. This weird upside-down world obviously suited her far better than it did me. Suddenly very curious, I leaned forward in my seat and said, 'And what about my brothers and my mum? How are they? Are they out in LA too?'

Showbiz Sibyl smiled. 'Your brothers are fine.' Her smile grew more thoughtful. 'And your mum is doing OK. I'm sure – with each day that passes – she'll be even more OK. But why are you asking if they're in LA? They're living in the exact same house that they've always lived in – the one you grew up in. Where else would they be?'

I felt my face go hot and I spluttered, 'Er . . . I dunno. I just thought . . .'

Sibyl smiled again. 'You just thought they'd be fixed up with a neat and easy dream ending as well, didn't you? Well, it ain't always as simple as that. But let me tell you something, Ronni, love. When the going gets tough,

the tough keep on going. We can't all run away to Wonderland, can we?'

I put my hand over my eyes and closed them for a moment. My face was hotter than ever. Showbiz Sibyl was one seriously weird chat-show host. If only I could have, I'd definitely have changed the channel to something more normal.

Showbiz Sibyl stood up, faced the audience and said, 'And now, ladies and gentleman, what time is it?'

As one, the audience roared, 'It's time for tea!'

'That's right,' said Showbiz Sibyl. 'It's always teatime.'

At the other end of the studio, a door opened and a boy appeared, pushing a silver tea trolley. From my armchair, I could see he had tufty black hair and a cute dimply face. A load of the audience broke out into a chorus of oooohs and ahhhhs.

A girl in the front row called out, 'Ohmigod! That little boy is soooo goooooorrrrrrrgeous.'

I looked over and, with a jolt, I realized I recognized her. It was Hannah-Michelle Peach. The girl who never has a bad word to say about anyone.

A voice right next to her shouted, 'Yeah – unlike

the hag in the hot seat!'

Hannah-Michelle Peach laughed. She might as well have floored me with a ninja kick.

Struggling to keep my hurt hidden, I looked to see who it was that had called me a hag. It was Tamika Hardwick. But that didn't surprise me much. Being a bitch is what she does best.

With a sinking heart, I scanned the other faces in the audience. And I saw that I recognized them too. All of them. I knew every single person in every single seat. And they knew me. We'd sat in assembly together. We'd sung songs together. We'd played tag together. We'd baked cakes together. Some of us had even known each other since we were three years old and played in the same sandpit at the same playgroup. And now they'd all piled into a television studio to watch me sink.

But there were two people missing. Crossing my fingers, I searched the rows of faces one more time. And then I uncrossed my fingers and breathed out a big sigh of relief. My friends Flooky and Kelly Bugg were not among them. My heart lifted up a little.

The boy arrived with the tea trolley. I looked at him

and with a sad, apologetic little smile, I said, 'Hey, Ryan.'

Nothing was surprising me now.

Without a word, my very own Number One Brother parked his trolley next to Showbiz Sibyl. Then he looked down at the floor and rushed back towards the studio exit.

My eyesight fuzzed up again. 'Come back,' I whispered. But he didn't hear me. He was already too far away.

Showbiz Sibyl stood up, reached over to the trolley and placed two cups on a low table between us. Then, tilting the teapot, she filled one cup for herself before passing the teapot to me. 'Pour your own,' she said. 'It's bad luck if I do it.'

Without a word, I did as I was told.

Sibyl lifted her own cup, moved it through the air in slow careful circles so that the tea sploshed around inside and then raised it to her lips and downed the whole lot in one big noisy slurp. Then she nodded at my cup and – in a freaky dreamy voice – said, 'And now you.'

I picked up my cup, jiggled it about a bit and took a sip. The tea was stone cold. Deep down, I always knew it would be. I drank it quickly.

Showbiz Sibyl wagged her finger at me and I gave her back my cup.

Placing the cup on the table in front of her, she stared down into it and, as she stared, she began muttering to herself and rocking backwards and forwards.

I held my breath.

So did the audience.

Showbiz Sibyl said,

'Ha!'

'Crikey!'

'Aha!'

'Ooooooh.'

'Well I never.'

'Hmmmm.'

And then she stopped rocking, sat back in her chair and said, 'Fair enough!'

'What is it?' I said. 'What did the tea leaves say?'

Showbiz Sibyl looked up at me. 'We can't calm the waves, but we can steer the ship.'

I stared at her. 'What?'

Sibyl shrugged. 'That's what it says. We can't calm the waves, but we can steer the ship.'

'But that's just a load of old rubbish,' I said. I was starting to feel really agitated. 'What the heck does it mean?'

Sibyl said, 'Don't get annoyed with me, dear. I just read the leaves. Have a look yourself if you don't believe me.' And she handed the cup back to me.

I stared into it and frowned. In the drop of water left in the very bottom of the cup, I could see hundreds and hundreds of tiny brown tea leaves. Nothing else. I frowned again and started to pass the cup back to her, but Sibyl said, 'Look again. And this time, look properly.'

So, with a sigh, I looked again. And just when I thought I was totally beyond surprises, I noticed that the tea leaves were all moving ever so slightly.

I lowered my face closer to the cup and stared harder.

In the dregs of my tea, the tea leaves were spinning round and round, faster and faster. They were spinning so fast that it was almost impossible to see them moving.

I noticed another very strange thing. The water was moving too. All by itself. As I watched, it trembled and tumbled and seethed and shuddered and heaved and shimmered and splashed and crashed and was making the

tea leaves spin faster and faster and faster.

'Weird,' I whispered.

Right under my nose, the undrunk drop of water
began to get bigger and bigger. Either that or the
teacup was getting smaller and smaller. Because – within
seconds – the sides of the teacup had completely vanished
and all I could see was water. Miles and miles and miles of
it. And it was sparkling and shimmering and shining and
twinkling and full of spinning dancing brown tea leaves.

'Weirder and weirder,' I whispered.

Panicking, I looked up so that I could ask Showbiz
Sibyl what it meant. But she'd vanished. And when I
looked around, the studio audience had vanished too.
And with an enormous stomach-sinking jolt of horror, I
realized I was all by myself. It was

just
me.

Being buffeted by the waves
in a sea of tea leaves.

And without a mobile phone to call for help. Without even a lilo to float on.

'Oh my God,' I said. 'What the heck is happening?' Frantically, I kicked my legs to stop myself from sinking beneath the crashing brown waves and spun round and round in the water in search of a place of safety. And far away in the distance – beyond the big grey watery splodge of a coastline – I saw something I recognized.

It was the grey outlines of cranes.

My heart jumped. I peered harder through the fog. And this time I saw the grey outlines of office blocks. My heart jumped a little higher.

The fog cleared and now I could see the grey shapes of thousands and thousands and thousands of metal shipping containers.

'Big whoop,' I said. And I meant it too. I meant it more than anything I've ever meant in my entire life.

Shielding my eyes to avoid the spray from the waves, I continued to search the coastline. There was something else I desperately needed to see. It was just one small detail. But it was a detail that was vitally important. If

And, if you haven't done
so already, I now need you
to turn this book sideways
and flick forward until
you find page 326.

Because an experience
as mad as the one I've
just described makes you
see the world in a totally
different way.

I could only see it, I'd know that everything was going
to be all right . . .

And suddenly there it was. Cutting through the
murky greyness like a shining beacon of hope was a small
jet of bright orange flame that flashed and flickered from
the top of a tall metal pipe.

'I want to go home now,' I whispered.

Very close to my face, a voice said, 'What?'

'I want to go home,' I said louder.

'Yes,' shouted the voice. 'She is OK!'

And then a hand took hold of mine and pulled me out
of the water.

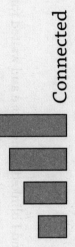

Connected

Someone

I was in a strange place. All around me was a sea of stars. They shone and glittered and sparkled and gleamed and twinkled and dazzled and flashed and burned with the brightest and whitest light I'd ever seen.

'Ouch,' I said. And then I blinked furiously and shook my head. The stars raced through the darkness like comets and were replaced at once by a single flickering glow of orange. For a second, it was the only speck of colour I could see. I stared at it and whispered, 'I want to go home now.'

Very close by, a voice said, 'What?'

'I want to go home,' I said again. And I blinked some more and waited for the world to stop spinning. And while I waited I kept very still and just carried on floating in outer space. Until, finally, I lifted one hand and covered my eyes. But I kept my other hand just where it was. Safe and warm inside someone else's.

Someone else's . . . ?

Somebody was holding my hand.

I froze.

But then I got curious. So I spread the fingers of my free hand and peeped through the gaps.

Staring straight down at me was a pair of worried grey eyes.

I snapped my fingers shut again and curled up into a defensive prickly ball. It wasn't that they weren't nice eyes. They were. Even in that fraction of a second, I got the distinct impression that they were very very nice eyes. It's just that I hadn't been expecting to see them. Certainly not at such close range anyway.

'Yes. That was very idiot thing to do,' said a second voice. Then there was a loud sniff. 'This is why we have important safety rule about head-on bumping.'

Startled, my body curled up tighter. Where were all these voices coming from?

A third voice demanded, 'What the heck did you do that for?'

This was weird. Way too weird! There seemed to be voices everywhere. I spread my fingers again and had another peep. There were now three pairs of eyes looking down on me. And somewhere, high above them, an orange light was flashing and flickering. I heard myself groan. Then I turned my head and looked around. And straight away, I stopped groaning and smiled. I knew where I was. I was flat on my back on Reggie Branning's dodgem track.

'Ouch,' I said again. And then I almost laughed. Because it was starting to make sense. 'We can't calm the waves but we can steer the ship,' I said to no one in particular. I was so excited I practically shouted it.

All three pairs of eyes narrowed. The voices – in reverse order to before – said,

'Zing! What the heck is she talking about?'

'Yes but are you feeling OK, Ronni? You are acting like very strange abnormal person.'

'Yes. Your idiot friend may need to see paramedic.'

I stopped smiling. *Had someone just called me an abnormal idiot?* I was about to say something, but then a picture popped into my head. It was a picture of me deliberately crashing headlong into Stuart Bolan. I saw that picture as clearly as if it was a still image in a slide show. It wasn't pretty.

Cringing, I clamped my jaw closed again and muttered, 'I'm fine.' And then I lifted my head so that I could see whose hand was still clinging on to mine.

Yuri Maximovich Krolik instantly let go of me, bunched his own hands into tight fists and shoved those fists firmly into his pockets. With a secret smile, I noticed that his cheeks had turned into two blotchy dollops of burning red. He looked like his own walking work of blob art. But *this* self-portrait didn't come with a smile. Instead, Yuri's forehead had crumpled into a big dark frown. 'Yes,' he said, quite crossly, 'I was worrying that you are killed.'

Normally I don't like being frowned at. But on this occasion, I think I probably deserved it.

'Sorry,' I said. 'But it's OK. I'm fine. Honestly I am.' And then *I* frowned too. 'How long have I been lying here?'

Yuri looked at me blankly.

I tried a different question. 'How long was I unconscious?'

Yuri still looked blank. His forehead crumpled even more and he scratched his head. Then he shot a quick glance at his brother Misha – but Misha was looking equally confused. Even Stuart Bolan looked unsure of himself. But only for a second. Because then, his mouth curled into a grin and he rocked back on his heels and started to snigger. The next moment, he was sniggering so hard that I thought somebody must actually have said something funny. And then he stopped sniggering and said,

'Ronni Runny Nose, you are such a random freak!'

And in a story stuffed full of very weird details, this is the weirdest one of all: practically every girl I know fancies Stuart Bolan. It's a popularly held belief that he's the coolest dude in our school. More than that, it's a commonly shared opinion that he's the most gorgeous guy in our town. More than that, it's a widespread assumption that he's the buffest boy in Great Britain. And more than that, it's a generally accepted view that he's the smoothest operator in the whole blinking world.

But I don't agree.

Not any more.

Yesterday, I finally took off my idiot goggles and found myself looking at a real douchebag.

Sometimes it takes a bump on the head to make you see sense.

Pushing my palms against the dirty dodgem track, I struggled up into a more dignified position. Then I looked Stuart straight in the eye and said, 'Will you stop calling me Runny Nose and will you stop calling me a freak? My name is Ronni Runnacles.' I thought about it a moment more and added, 'Actually, Stuart, can you quit using the word freak full stop? It's not nice.'

Stuart raised his eyebrows. But only for a second. Because then he flicked his bottle-bleached fringe out of his face, puckered up his lips into a big flirty pout and blew me a kiss. And then he winked and said, 'I know you're joking, Ronni Runny Nose. You think I'm well nice. Everyone does.'

I sighed.

Stuart's grin faded a little. 'You *are* joking, right?'

'No,' I said. 'I'm not joking. I think you need to be nicer, Stuart. I really do.' And then I bit my lip and blushed because I knew that he wasn't the only one capable of behaving like a douchebag. For the past month, I'd been doing a mighty fine impression of a premium douchebag myself.

Stuart Bolan's grin disappeared completely and he stared at me in total astonishment. But only for a second. And then he lifted his lip up into a sneer and said the only thing that he could apparently think of to say. '*Zing!*'

I shrugged my shoulders and sighed again. 'Zing? Yeah . . . whatever *that* means.'

Stuart's sneer got bigger. His lip curled higher and higher and his eyebrows sunk lower and lower and – right in front of my eyes – his entire face collapsed in on itself until it was barely any bigger than the size of a 2p coin. For somebody so good-looking, he'd done a really top job of making himself ming as much as Ming the Merciless. 'Vinditious freaking freak,' he snapped. And with that, he stood up, angrily brushed the dust off his skinny grey jeans, flicked us a V sign and stropped off. But just before he disappeared behind the queue for the chair-o-planes, he turned and shouted, 'And I flipping hate foreigners.' And then he was gone.

Sometimes there's really very little left to say. Misha just said it anyway. 'Yes,' he said with a sniff. 'This boy is a bum hole.' And although it was harsh, I guess that comment must have expressed the popularly held belief and commonly shared opinion and widespread assumption and generally accepted view of everyone present because neither me nor Yuri disagreed.

But I couldn't be bothered to linger over the topic of Stuart Bolan. He wasn't important. I had questions that still needed answers. 'How long was I unconscious?'

Yuri looked confused again. 'Yes but why do you ask this? I am not aware you have any losses of consciousness.'

Misha said, 'Yes. As soon as you have prohibited head-on bumping crash, I am stopping the power and I am coming straight over to check you are not horribly injured, mutilated or dead. And here you are with no horrible injury or obvious mutilation . . . and I am thinking you are alive . . . yes?'

I stared at both of them. 'But . . . but . . . I've been . . .' I struggled for the right word, 'I've been . . . *away* . . . for at least a couple of days.'

Yuri shook his head and gave me an odd smile. 'You haven't been anywhere. You are all the time here on dodgem track.'

'But . . . but . . .' I found myself struggling again. 'My eyes must have been closed? I must have been lying here . . . not moving?'

Yuri shrugged. 'You have eyes shut for five seconds. Maybe six seconds.'

Misha sniffed and nodded. 'Yes. Maybe seven seconds.'

'But it's just not possible.' I couldn't keep the astonishment from creeping into my voice.

'Since the crash . . . a lot has happened! I've done things. I've been places. I've talked to people.' I looked at Yuri. 'I talked to you!'

Misha sniffed and nodded at his brother. 'Yes. I am thinking your crazy friend needs medical head-check from expert paramedic. I will make emergency telephone call.' And with that, he upped and walked off to his ticket kiosk.

Yuri watched him leave and then his anxious grey eyes flicked back to mine.

'I'm fine,' I protested. And to be fair, I was fine. Everything was still intact. Everything seemed to be working OK. Everything felt normal. Even my Himalayas seemed completely unbothered by the collision, and those two lumpy ladies have been weirding me out in a big way for months. The only thing that *wasn't* OK was my understanding of what had just happened. I couldn't get my head around it at all.

Everything suddenly seemed massively complicated.

Maybe the mind is like that.

Yuri pushed his mousy hair away from his eyes and looked at me. I shivered. I could see the sky and the sea and the whole world in those eyes. 'Yes,' he said gently, 'I am thinking you are having a mix-up of imagination and reality. Perhaps you have been reading too many intense novels.' And then he smiled at me and, immediately, I felt warm and happy. It was like the sun had peeped out from behind a cloud and lit up his entire face.

And all of a sudden, I was thinking about my nan. And in particular, I was thinking about her amazing ability to be almost always right. My nan has this thing she says about smiles. Until yesterday, I thought it was just a load of spreadable

easy-squeeze

full-fat

foil-wrapped

vacuum-packed

extra-mature

cheese.

But now I know it's a rock-solid fact.

Because when it's done properly, you can't give away a smile. It always comes back to you.

I beamed back at Yuri. 'I'm sorry I behaved like a real douchebag on the dodgem track. It won't happen again.'

Yuri laughed. And it wasn't a shallow snigger of the Stuart Bolan variety. It was a laugh as deep and as warm as a bubble bath. 'Yes,' he said. 'You are right. Brother Misha says you have lifetime ban from dodgem cars.'

'Whoop,' I said. I didn't really mean it. But then again, I wasn't actually being sarcastic either. The word had just popped out of my mouth before I'd had a chance to clear it with my brain. In all honesty, a dodgem ban seemed perfectly reasonable in the circumstances.

Just then, Misha returned. 'Yes. Expert paramedic person will come to check your head to see if you have harmful brain damages.'

I scrambled to my feet. 'Whoa! Hang on,' I said. 'I'm OK. It was . . . it was nothing.'

Misha looked doubtful.

'Honestly,' I pleaded. 'I felt a bit weird for a few seconds, that's all. I saw a few stars and I totally showed myself up. But I'm really OK now. I am. Or I'm going to be. Honestly.'

Misha still looked doubtful. Yuri did too.

'I seriously do not need my head checking by any expert paramedic,' I said. I was starting to panic. What the heck would a paramedic say if I started talking about all the stuff that had happened in those five or six or seven seconds when my eyes were closed? What would anybody say? And right then and there, I made a decision. I wouldn't tell anyone. I'd keep it to myself and I'd quietly put it all down to experience and learn something from it.

'I should go home,' I said. 'My mum and my nan will be worrying about me, and my brothers Ryan, Jack and Joe like it when I referee their ninja wars, and my baby brother Harrison goes to bed really early and I like to see him before he's asleep.' And then I looked at my watch and remembered that it was still ages until Harrison's bedtime and that school hadn't even finished.

Yuri said something to Misha in Russian. Misha sniffed, looked at me sternly and said, 'Yes but you make solemn promise to see professional doctor if you are feeling ill.'

'Yes,' I said. 'I solemnly promise.'

Misha sniffed again. 'Don't come back to dodgem track. Lifetime ban.' And with those crystal-clear parting words, he walked off.

Yuri picked up his bag and put the strap across his forehead. But then he seemed to think better of it, reddened and moved the strap down to his shoulder. Then he looked at me. 'Yes but you also made solemn promise to come with me back to school. And I am not wanting to be even more late. I am wanting to learn about fat king Henry Eight in history lesson.'

And as he said this, I realized with quite a lot of shock that I wanted to get back to school too. Because I have a lot of unfinished business there. Like my education for starters. The truth is that the last month has been a total mess. And it's about time I started seriously focusing again or next year I could be sitting in a classroom all by myself reading Topsy and Tim books.

And then there's Flooky and Bugg. They're my best friends. I've known them since we were all three years old and went to the same playgroup. And over the years, we've played Burnout together, driven dodgems together, eaten ice creams on the seafront together and stood side by side in front of a booing audience and sung 'Pokerface' together. They're the best friends I could ever ask for. They are certainly not the type to sit by and watch me sink. But just recently I've pushed them so far away that they've practically disappeared off the page. And they're not the only ones. I've done that to everyone. I think it's because I've been worried about being let down. But that's no way to live. You must trust people or life becomes impossible.

And finally there's the small issue of Sadie Slowgrove.

Over the past month, I've been rotten to her. She's been pretty rancid right back. To be fair, I think the situation has been one that neither of us has been able to comfortably bask in. One month ago, my dad left my mum and my brothers and me and ran away to Scotland with Sadie Slowgrove's mum. And apart from one postcard of a random bagpiper and a scary solicitor's letter which made my mum cry, we haven't heard from him since.

Crap like that sort of changes the way you look at the world.

But it's hardly Sadie's fault. This was simply one of life's rougher waves and I bet Sadie and her dad were just as knocked off balance by it as me and my family were. Now there's nothing to be done but try to steer ourselves through it and get on with our lives.

It took me a month to work this out. The thoughts all hit me at once as I stood with Yuri on the dodgem track. They came as a relief. It's not nice keeping a whole load of anger locked away inside. It gives you bellyache.

'We better get moving,' I said. And I let Yuri Maximovich Krolik lead the way out of Reggie Branning's Amusement Park and walked with him back to our school.

And although that brings me to the end of my story about the very weird thing that happened yesterday, there's still a tiny bit more to tell. Because early this morning, there was a knock on the front door of my house. I was still in bed. Last night, I told my mum and my nan that I won't ever be late for school again and I meant it. But as today is a Saturday and as I'm not naturally an early bird, I wasn't in any big rush to move. Dimly, I heard the knock-knock-knock. And then I heard the doorbell. And then – a few seconds later – I heard the thump of feet on the stairs.

'Ronni, that weird boy from school is outside. He wants to talk to you!'

It was my Number One Brother, Ryan. I flipped back the top of my duvet and sat up in shock. Ryan was leaning against my door frame with his arms folded and a snarky smirk spreading across his face. He looked just like a big fat irritating smugster. Even so, I still wouldn't divorce myself from being his sister. Not ever.

Eventually, I found my brain and managed to say, *'What* weird boy?'

'The one who carries his bag round on his head,' said Ryan. 'The foreign one.'

'He's not foreign,' I said. 'He's Russian.' And then I thought about it a moment more and added, 'And he's not weird either. He's nice.'

Ryan's face lit up. 'Ooooohhhhh. Ronni and Spaceman sitting by the sea . . . K.I.S.S.I.N.G.'

'His name is Yuri,' I said. 'Get him into the kitchen and tell him I'll be down in five minutes.'

And then I picked up my pillow and hurled it as hard as I could at Ryan's head.

I've never got myself sorted so quickly. It's amazing what you can do if you relax your bathroom routine a bit. All you really need is a quick splash at the sink and a squirt of Impulse. Then you chuck on your favourite pair of skinny pink jeans, a pair of tiger-print Converse, a T-shirt with a picture of a pug on it, a sloppy grey cardigan and tie back your hair with your favourite reliable scrunchy. And you're there.

Bingo Bango!

If I hadn't wasted an entire minute looking for my phone, I'd have probably been Good To Go in four minutes flat. I've no idea what I ever did in the bathroom that took me so long.

When I got downstairs, Yuri was sitting in the kitchen talking to my mum. For one horrible second, I panicked and hoped that he hadn't told her anything about yesterday or the fact that I'd ducked out of school. But, as it happened, they were having a completely harmless conversation about books. I breathed a huge sigh of relief. And then, straight away, I breathed an even bigger one when I realized that my mum was actually dressed for once. She even had some make-up on and was smiling. It was such a rare and fantastic sight that I had to look twice to make sure I hadn't imagined it. And then when I saw that I hadn't and that this was actually happening I smiled too.

My mum glanced up, saw me and beamed. 'Hi, Ronni. Yuri has been telling me that you're both in the same English class and that you're off to the town library this morning to do some homework on Lewis Carroll.'

My smile froze. 'On who?'

'Lewis Carroll,' said Yuri quickly. 'Intense writer of classic nonsense novel *Alice's Adventures in Wonderland*.' And then he went a little bit blotchy, stared at me very intently with those incredible grey eyes and said, 'We agree to do homework together, remember?'

'Oh y-e-a-h,' I said.

'I think that's a great idea,' said my mum, still beaming. 'Homework is always more fun when you do it with a partner. I remember reading *Alice in Wonderland* when I was at school. On the surface, it seems like a load of old silliness, but actually that book is quite deep. It's all about life being a sequence of meaningless puzzles and stuff like that.'

I looked at my mum, surprised. 'I didn't know you knew all that. You thought I was reading *Black Beauty* yesterday!'

My mum's beam broke. 'Only because that's what *you* told me!'

Just then, the kitchen door opened and my nan appeared. She was holding Harrison with one hand and a Nerf gun with the other. She looked at us and said, 'Ladies, you're not belly-aching again, are you? I've got a hot date this morning. I want to be leaving this house in a relaxed frame of mind.' And then she saw Yuri and said, 'Oh! Pardon me. I didn't realize we had company.'

Yuri nodded his head, held out his hand and said, 'Yes. I am Yuri Maximovich Krolik. Delighted to meet you.'

My nan turned an extreme shade of pink, nodded her head back at him and said, 'Oh!

Likewise, Mr Chronic.' And then she looked at me, winked and said, 'Honk!'

I put my head down to hide my horror, fished my phone out of my pocket and tweeted . . .

Ronni Runnacles @ronneee_r

My nan is totally embarrassing me. She just called my friend *Mr Chronic*. #shame #truth

Yuri smiled. 'Yes. But actually my name is Yuri Maximovich Krolik. K-r-o-l-i-k. It is Russian name.'

'Ooooh,' said my nan. 'That's nice. Krolik. Does that mean anything?'

Yuri's smile grew. 'Yes. It means rabbit. Krolik is Russian word for rabbit.' And then he frowned a little and said, 'What does Runnacle mean?'

'Runnacles,' said me, my nan and my mum all at once.

Yuri nodded. 'Yes. Sorry. What does Runnacles mean?'

My nan and my mum and I looked at each other. And then my nan said, 'Well, don't ask me! It's not my name. I'm a Herbert and proud of it.' Putting her Nerf gun down on the worktop, she passed Harrison to my mum before adding, 'Anyway, I've got to be getting on. I mustn't keep my gentleman friend waiting.'

My mum smiled. 'Ooooh! Who is he?'

'Oh, it's only Ken from the computer club,' replied my nan. 'He's been badgering me to go for a walk in the park with him for ages. He reckons the flowers smell lovely this time of year.' And then she looked at me and said, 'What's up with you, lady?'

A loud squeak had escaped from my mouth. Everybody in the kitchen was staring at me. Even Harrison was looking at me, and he makes these kinds of noises all the time. 'Nothing's up, Nan,' I said. 'It's just that there's a whole line of older ladies who'd love him to squeeze their toothpaste. Have a lovely time and – whatever you do – don't mess it up!'

My nan looked annoyed. 'Oooh, you cheeky minx! Less of the older, thank you. I'm in my prime.' And then she smiled at Yuri again, said, 'Lovely to meet you, Mr Chronic,' and left the kitchen.

My mum jiggled Harrison on her lap, gave a little laugh and said, 'We still haven't told Yuri what a Runnacle is. I haven't got a clue. Have you, Ronni?'

'Nope,' I said. 'But I know we've got more than one of them.' And then I stared at Yuri very intently and added, 'Come on, we should be going. We've got loads of homework to do.' And taking my remarkable white rabbit by the arm, I steered him out of the kitchen and through the hallway and followed him out of the front door and into a whole new day.

As soon as we were outside and a safe distance from the house, I said, 'We're not actually going to the library, are we?'

Yuri shrugged. 'Yes but why not? We can if you like. It is nice place.' He pushed a lock of hair away from his beautiful eyes and added, 'And afterwards, we can go to seafront and I will buy you doughnut. But, really, I am wanting to know that you are OK after yesterday and that you do not have delayed brain-damage trauma like Misha says you have.'

I smiled. 'I don't. But please tell Misha that I'm touched by his concern.' And then my face burned a bit and I said, 'Actually, Yuri, I'm touched by *your* concern too.'

Yuri's eyes sparkled with mischief. He nodded at something he could see behind me and said, 'Yes but now your face is looking like flame from waste pipe over there.'

I turned. Through the gaps between the houses, I could see a backdrop of ships and cranes and metal containers. And leaping out from this familiar scene was the orange flame I always look for from my bedroom window. And which – without fail – I always find.

'That flame is burning off waste gas,' I said to Yuri. 'If it ever went out, we'd all explode. BOOM.'

Yuri's smile grew. 'Yes. You say some funny things, Ronni Runnacle, and you are making me laugh.' And then his face turned flame-coloured too and he said, 'I am liking you very much.'

I stared at him. 'Really?' Hope swelled up inside me. 'You seriously like me? Stupid boring Ronni Runnacles?' And before I could stop myself, I said, 'Even the tide wouldn't take *me* out.'

Yuri's forehead crumpled into the emperor of all frowns. 'I like you,' he insisted. 'I really do.' And then – as if to prove his point – he leaned forward and kissed me gently on the lips. And it felt kind of like being touched by a single second of intense wonderland sunshine.

But better.

Because it was definitely and delightfully and deliciously real.

Ronni Runnacles @ronneee_r

@Flooky @kellylikesdoughnuts Loads to tell you! #wheretostart

HAPPY SUMMER DAYS AHEAD :-) XXXXX

Acknowledgements

I'm going to use this page to say a fat thank-you to . . .

Rachel Petty at
Macmillan Children's Books

and

Joanna Deveraux
at Pollinger

and

Lauren Ace
who's also at Macmillan

and

Becky MacNaughton
who read some early ideas

and
Hayley Yeeles who did too

and
my niece, Emma, who is
NOT a douchebag!

and
Donna Hansell
who played 2p Coin Shove with me

and
Paston Sixth Form College,
Norfolk

and
GT, as always. x

WHAT'S UP WITH JODY BARTON?

Hayley Long

Hey, Reader!

Have you ever fallen in love
so fast with someone so random
that it makes your head spin?

If yes, you should totally read this book.

If no, you should totally read this book.

Because I'm about to let you into
a huge secret, one that even my
twin sister doesn't know about.
It's epically messing with my brain.

Stand by as I prepare to spill
some seriously intense beans...

Jody

am I JeaLOus that mY Best frIeND has a BOYfrIeND? DOes that meaN I'm traGIC??? Is mY CurreNt haIr COLOur (meLODY DeeP PLum) Better thaN that DODGY CustarD COLOur I trIeD Last week?

PerhaPs I ShOuLD GO Out wIth Gareth stINGeCOmBe — eveN thOuGh I DON't faNCY hIm the Least tINIest BIt. If I DON't faNCY Gareth stINGeCOmBe the Least tINIest BIt, whY am I OBsessING aBOut hIs maNLY thINGs?

these BOOks are aBOut aLL the ImPOrtaNt QuestIONs IN LIfe. theY're DefINIteLY NOt aBOut sIttING IN mY warDrOBe Or havING a meNtaL DIsturBaNCe Of aNY kIND . . .